PALE HEARTS

Emily Eckart

PALE HEARTS Copyright © 2016 by Emily Eckart. All Rights Reserved. Printed in the United States of America. No part of this book may be used or reproduced in any manner whatsoever without written permission except brief quotations. For information, contact Insomnia Publishing, 11 Avery Rd, Londonderry, NH 03053

Cover image designed by E. Prybylski.

www.insomnia-publishing.com

ISBN-10:0986397555

ISBN-13:9780986397554

Some stories in this book previously appeared in the following publications: "Hiding Game" in Corium Magazine; "Counterpoint" in Gravel; "An Inquiry into the Nature of Happiness" in Jelly Bucket; "The Beech Tree" in Literary Orphans; "Man and Machine" in Nature; "Depthless" in New World Writing; "The Grechtzoar" in Potomac Review; "The Way You Cover" in The Literary Yard; "Incompatible Truths" in The Summerset Review; "Peanut Butter" in Tower Journal.

ACKNOWLEDGMENTS

I am indebted to Elizabeth Prybylski, Joshua Quivey, and the staff of Insomnia Publishing for their fantastic work editing and producing this book.

I am also grateful to Ashley Bray, Brenda Dion, and Sarah Farren, who critiqued endless drafts of these stories.

My teachers Margaret Morganroth Gullette, Ron MacLean, and Chip Cheek provided much advice and guidance.

John and Connie Eckart supported me through all my endeavors.

Finally, I am thankful for the encouragement of Avery Yen, Ingrid Yen, Naho Zhu, Steven Max-Faults, Matthew Young, Amy Zhang, Ran Wei, and Thomas Luo.

To my parents and Tom

CONTENTS

THE BEECH TREE

Until I stood before her casket, Grandma was the only person I could not imagine dead. She'd looked as aged as ever when I saw her days before, a husk of raisin wrinkles, already so wizened, time could do nothing else. I thought she could live for centuries. But now she lay still in her woolen dress, her lucent eyes closed and her hands leathered and gray, like the bark of an ancient beech.

The dim room's air hung thick with the scent of white chrysanthemums. Mark stood behind me, always watching for signs of slippage. I leaned back against him, his body warm with concern. I could feel right through him, through membrane and muscle to dry, stiff bones beneath. His skin felt like an apple peel: too soft to stop the flesh from bruising and falling away.

Later that day, I sliced a pear in Grandma's kitchen. It had fallen to us to sort her things. The chrysanthemums stood in a vase on the table. Their scent reminded me of the beech flowers, blooming yellow in June. On weekends at Grandma's, I'd lean against the trunk and look up at the green dome of its branches. Back then, the bark was gray and smooth.

The beech tree stood behind Grandma's house. Mark had never seen it.

The knife slipped and sliced a sliver off the joint of my thumb. I gasped.

"Geez, Kacey," Mark said, rushing over to inspect. "You okay?"

"It was an accident."

He frowned, not believing in accidents. A drop of blood sat, glistening on the pear's pale snowy flesh.

I was ten when I started spending summers at Grandma's house. She and my mother didn't talk. It had to do with my grandfather, who died young, long before I was born. He survived World War II only to meet a mundane death at home: an icy curve, a slip of the wheel, an oak where his car left the road. My mother was nine years old at the time.

But no matter if Grandma continued cooking Grandpa's favorite meals long after he was dead; no matter if she bought men's shirts and hung them in her closet with the tags still on, or brought home books he would have liked—Trees of the World, The European Forest. Need trumped uncomfortable memories. My mother had to work and couldn't afford daycare when I was out of school in the summer. My aunt, who used to watch me, had moved away. At the end of fifth grade, my mother took me as soon as school let out and drove me the two hours to Grandma's.

I stood on the stoop of the brick house, listening to the raspy cries of cicadas. The door cracked open; cool air spilled from the darkness at its edge. Mom waved and drove away. Grandma swept me inside with my suitcase, and the door swung shut behind me.

Grandma wore a brown long-sleeved dress, her hair held back by silver bobby pins. She smiled, but did not come forward to hug me.

"You look just like your mother," she said. "A lot like your grandfather, too." She nodded, as if that decided it. "Come in. Dinner's ready."

I followed her down the narrow hallway. The dining room had a bay window and dark hardwood paneling. A glass-doored hutch, mostly empty, and a dining table covered with a white lace cloth filled the empty floor space. In the center of the table sat a plate of roast beef, surrounded by dishes of green beans, mashed potatoes, and corn. Three places were set at the table, the third plate covered by a thin sheet of dust.

"Sit down," she said, pulling out a chair. I left my suitcase next to the hutch. She carved the roast with a massive fork and knife. Her hands shook; the knife gleamed in the light. It had a beautiful serrated edge.

"This was one of your father's favorite dishes," she said.

"You mean my grandfather?" I asked. She paused and looked at me.

"Oh," she said. "Oh, yes." She sounded dubious. She put a thick slice of meat on my plate, much more than I could eat, and accompanied it with a generous scoop of beans, potatoes, and corn. She served herself, but put nothing on the third plate.

"How old are you?" she asked.

"Ten."

She sat down and smiled. "Ten." She said it as though the word were a poem in itself. "When I was that age, I loved to go exploring. The yard extends quite a ways. There used to be an arboretum in the back."

"A what?"

"A place where they grow all different trees from around the world, like a tree museum. Researchers went there to study them. That's how I met your father when I was just a few years older than you."

"You mean my grandfather?"

"I saw him one day, out by the back stone fence. He wanted to come see the beech tree. There was an old one in our yard, probably hundreds of years old. I invited him over. He said specimens like that are hard to find."

She had barely touched her food, while I had eaten as much as I could. The beef was tender, seeping with juice, and the vegetables were coated with butter, pepper, and salt. I had never eaten anything so superior to my mother's bland cooking.

"I think I'm done. Where should I put my suitcase?"

"You have a suitcase?" She seemed confused, but stood up. "In your room, I suppose."

I followed her down the hallway. Two doors stood across from each other, and a third door at the end. She opened one of the side doors. "This is your room. Don't you remember?"

Strangely enough, I felt as though I did. The bed had lavender sheets with a white floral print, and a desk and a shaded lamp stood in one corner. The room had an old, familiar smell, like clothes left in a drawer for a long time.

"You seem tired, Patty," she said. "You should rest. I'll take care of cleaning up." Her voice was gentle and patient, as my mother's never was. Kind wrinkles occupied the corners of her eyes. Her appearance, which had before looked plain, suddenly appeared elegant and beautiful. I admired her simple dress, her white hair held back by silver bobby pins. Despite her confusion, I decided I liked her.

Over the summers, I grew accustomed to her forgetfulness and how she called me by my mother's name. She drove to the grocery store each day, buying fresh ingredients for her elaborate meals. Grandma left in the morning, climbed into her ancient car, and backed down the long gravel driveway, going about five miles an hour. I stood by the front screen door and listen to the sound of her car fade, gradually overcome by songbirds and the stirring of the wind.

While she was gone, I had lots to explore. Besides her room and mine, there was the third room at the end of the hallway. I imagined a cool air seeped from under its door, as though it led to stone steps spiraling into underground darkness. One day, I tried the knob tentatively, and stood still as the door swung open.

The shades were closed, and it took my eyes a moment to adjust to the gray light. A desk, a bookshelf, and a bureau, all piled with papers and books huddled inside. A closet door occupied space in the corner. I made my way across the room and opened it. Inside hung men's shirts, and shoes sat on a rack in the bottom. Shirts that looked new hung in front, many with the tags still on. In the back, the shirts were soft; they smelled like dust and cedar. This room must have been my grandfather's.

When I could no longer breathe the stale air of my grandfather's study, I explored outside. Grandma's house sat at the edge of a tiny town, with the nearest neighbors miles away. The lawn resembled a meadow where I waded through tall grass, daisies, and Queen Anne's lace to the backyard. A stand of pine trees marked the edge about a quarter of a mile off. I went toward them, pausing to stare at spots where rabbits and chipmunks rustled in the undergrowth.

Behind the pines, I discovered a clearing bordered by a stout stone fence. In front of the fence stood an enormous tree with was no visible trunk. It looked like an exuberant garden shrub, grown to full capacity without humans snipping at its branches.

I pushed my way through the foliage and found myself a dim space, enclosed by branches sloping to the ground. The trunk presented a wide, almost flat surface, like a canvas. I rested my hand against the finely-textured gray bark, smooth like my own skin.

⸺∿⸺

Grandma returned around noon with bags and bags of groceries. I tried to help her put things away, but her cabinets had no discernible order. Flour fraternized with stewed tomatoes and olives; sugar sat in wanton repose with canned pineapple and bouillon cubes. The pattern always shifted, random new items replacing the ones that had been used. The only constant was the bottom shelf of one cupboard, which held a cardboard box filled with shards of dishes. Grandma said they were from her wedding set, and that she would have them fixed one day.

She made lamb with rosemary and garlic, duck with orange sauce, stewed beef. Each had been a favorite of my grandfather's. She said he had blond hair like mine and thick fingers, strong like the roots of trees. He especially loved the beech tree out back. It was because of that tree that they met. Grandma's story varied. Sometimes, she said, he invited her to come look at it; other times, it was that she beckoned to him. Either way, the tree was constant. At the beginning of their relationship, it was their meeting place. After they married, they would sit together on one of the low branches.

"Have you been out there?" I asked. "Recently?"

"No, not for many years."

"Why not?"

"I'm afraid it might have changed," she said, "since I saw it last."

I found her romantic, almost mythological. I couldn't imagine her existing in any other way. At home and at school, I thought of cursive script on envelopes, of book spines in weak light. I thought of gray bark as smooth and vulnerable as skin.

When I arrived each summer, the guest bedroom was set up for me with the lavender sheets she always used, soft and old-smelling as my grandfather's shirts. I

came to know the way my door creaked when it opened
. I knew the warp of the bookshelf and the shadows cast
by the lamp. In the desk, I discovered a stack of blank,
yellowed notecards. These, too, became mine.

As a teenager, a strange new sadness afflicted me, one
that enveloped my body like a film of gelid air. When I
looked at other people, I saw the skeletons beneath their
skins: pale calcium scaffolds, the only thing that would
outlast perished muscle and rotted brain. Inside each
person hid a smooth, white pile of bones. The image
came to me at odd moments: in the gym locker room,
while everyone lounged in sports bras; in the school
bathroom, when girls puckered into mirrors to apply lip
gloss. All of us would be consumed. I felt dizzy on the
school's wide lawn, where soon, we might be buried.

My grandfather in particular fascinated me. At
Grandma's that summer, when she was away, I spent
hours in his study. I sat down on the office chair, and
a cloud of dust rose around me. I read his research
papers and perused his books, as ancient to me as the
redwoods they described. I discovered a note to call the
arboretum written in his hand. I opened a drawer and
found an envelope addressed to Grandma in cursive. It
was empty. Then I saw the jewelry box. I lifted the lid,
covered with dull brown fabric. It dropped open faster
than I expected, and a lock of hair fell out. The hair was
soft, its blond unfaded. A cool thrill went through me: I
had just touched part of a dead person.

The hallway floor creaked. I rushed out of the study,
fumbling for an excuse. But Grandma still was not
home.

I went out back to climb the beech tree. I sat on one of
the thick branches with my back to the trunk and looked
up at the shifting leaves and caught the scent of autumn.
Though the air was warm, and the leaves still green, I

knew what would happen to them soon. They would turn brown and desiccated; they would tremble and fall away. I felt sorry for them. They would be ground into dust while the tree kept living; no one would remember them when it grew a new batch in the spring. I saw myself, too, rotting, festering flesh falling in slick chunks off the bone. The blue sky seemed so cruel. It would continue to exist after I dissolved in the earth—shining, unaltered, without me.

Back inside, I went into my room and opened my suitcase. I dug to the bottom and pulled out a pair of rolled-up sweat pants, shaking them out and picking up the X-Acto knife. I liked how precise the tip was. It made me think of a fine calligraphy pen with a nib perfect for writing.

I took off my shorts and sat with my legs spread apart, the blade held against the upper part of my thigh. I took a breath and exhaled as I gently parted the skin. The first one was always hardest. The white skin split; my mind rushed to the small line of pain. I sighed and did it again. Two small cuts, in parallel, a red drop welling from each.

I had cotton balls and disinfectant in my suitcase— hydrogen peroxide, which I loved for its exquisite sting. I dabbed some on the cuts and shut my eyes against the reassuring pain, the nerves wired and working, the flesh undoubtedly alive. I spread antibiotic cream on a Band-Aid and pressed it over the wound. The cool salve soothed me. Soon, like it had in other places, my skin would heal.

Later, Grandma returned with her groceries. I watched her mix a marinade, pour it over chunks of lamb, dice the eggplant and chop the rosemary. While the lamb stewed, she made a blueberry pie, layering the sweet mix with strips of crust she had rolled that morning. After dinner, we sat eating warm slices while listening to a record of stately, minor-key music—Handel, she said, my grandfather's favorite.

"Grandma?" I asked. "Do you ever feel like things are decaying? Right in front of you?"

She did not answer at first.

"That's what memory is for," she said. "So you can keep things as you like them."

If the years fell like leaves, she was the tree: solid, despite everything, and lasting.

I did it because of a boy. I was twenty-one and had not visited Grandma for two years. There were internships to apply for, research papers to complete. I started dating the boy when I was a sophomore. Because it lasted for a year, I thought it would last forever.

Perhaps he was just as desperate for friendship as I was. That would explain why he waited twelve full months to take my shorts off, a mistake that proved my downfall.

He was kissing my leg when he saw the scars on my upper thighs. I had completely forgotten about them. They were as familiar to me as my eyebrows and fingernails. The oldest were faint and mostly healed. But the new ones were brown with tiny scabbed ridges, like freshly piled dirt marking a grave.

He started back with a look of concern. In that brief moment, I imagined he would ask what had happened. I would consider lying, but would choose trust, and would tell him everything. He would wonder why I did it. I would explain how I felt bad, really bad sometimes, and it was strange, but the cutting helped.

That was not what happened. He didn't say anything. He resumed with some distracted kisses, and then remembered he had a paper to write. He withdrew quietly from my life, becoming more and more absent. When I finally asked if he wanted to end it, he shrugged.

That summer, I did no internships. I went to Grandma's, just as I used to. When I arrived, her hair looked thinner than before, but the kind crinkles around her eyes remained alongside the dazed warmth in her voice like no time had passed. I was Patty, and Grandpa was still alive, about to come home any minute.

Her arms trembled as she hugged me. I wondered what she would think of my silly life, of the box cutter I carried in my purse. I drew away sooner than I should have, ashamed.

She went to bed at eight o' clock. It was a warm June evening, still light at that hour, so I went to see the tree. I knew it waited loyally, as people never did.

I waded through the grass in the back and pushed through the branches, through its green leaves that looked so new. I remembered each root, knot, and branch. I sat on a low limb, loneliness tightening my throat. The box cutter's weight in my pocket reassured me. I came out planning to cut myself there. Maybe the tree would appreciate my blood, would absorb it and use it like water, for growth.

My hand brushed against the bark, and it felt so smooth, like paper to be written on. I took out the knife and slid open the blade, making just a small cut at first: a little line in gray, a mark to prove I had been here. I widened the gash, little bits of bark peeling away like apple skin. Before I knew it, the lines became letters.

K, A, C.

I stabbed and slashed, tearing out hunks of bark, letters proliferating before my eyes. I am here, I thought with each letter. I exist, however briefly.

KACEY. KACEY. KACEY.

Sap glistened where I sliced the skin. There, I thought. It will be there forever. My etched name, eternal, unlike me.

It was easy to avoid her. I invented needy friends, brutal classes, crucial interviews. I graduated and started work without ever visiting her. It wasn't until I got engaged to Mark, two years out of school, that I went to Grandma's again. He wanted to meet her, this woman I spoke of so frequently. I hadn't realized I talked so much about her. There was no reason I could tell him for delaying a visit, so we climbed into my car and drove to her place for a weekend.

We arrived on a September evening when the sun was just setting. The house remained the same, a constant in a changing world. The front door was unlocked and asters bloomed in the vase on the counter. The same glass-doored hutch, and the familiar white lace table cloth filled the dining room. I expected to see Grandma in her favorite brown wool dress. But she was nowhere to be found.

Mark brought our suitcases inside while I went out back. I called for her.

"Grandma?"

We had seen her car in the driveway, so where could she have gone? She was eighty-five and fragile. I wondered if she became one of those elders who wandered, if we'd find her by the side of a highway ten miles from here.

"Grandma?" For some reason, I walked toward the beech tree. I fought through the grass, nearly tripping on sticks and roots in the fading light. When I reached the tree, I slipped through the draping branches and saw a hunched silhouette.

Her skin had grown more wrinkled, and new spots decorated her face. Her hair hung thin and limp. Her bones, I knew, were frail.

"I saw the picture you mailed," she said. "He looks just like your father."

I didn't want her to say that. It sounded like an omen that Mark would be taken from me—that I would be made alone, like her.

"He proposed here, under this tree."

"You shouldn't have come out here," I said. My voice was loud and defensive. "You could've fallen."

"I knew it might have changed," she sighed. "But I couldn't bear not to see it, just once more before I die."

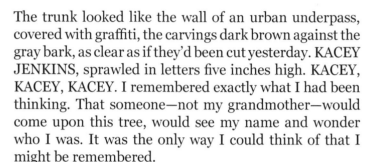

The trunk looked like the wall of an urban underpass, covered with graffiti, the carvings dark brown against the gray bark, as clear as if they'd been cut yesterday. KACEY JENKINS, sprawled in letters five inches high. KACEY, KACEY, KACEY. I remembered exactly what I had been thinking. That someone—not my grandmother—would come upon this tree, would see my name and wonder who I was. It was the only way I could think of that I might be remembered.

Grandma looked small, like she had shrunk inside her skin.

"I'm tired," she said. "Let's go inside."

Turning away, I walked her back to the house.

THE SAFETY APP

"I don't want to do this to Aidan," Phil said. "It's wrong."

Ramona sighed as she dusted the dining room hutch. She lifted a family picture and swept a damp paper towel underneath, bringing up a few specks of dust. Do this to Aidan—as though it weren't a shot for their son's safety but some kind of risky surgery. She glanced at the picture as she set it back down: a portrait of the whole family taken three years ago. Back then, she and Phil had worn broad smiles. Her face had been smooth, free of worry lines.

Over the last year, Phil transformed from a partner into a rival, and she couldn't understand his resistance. Didn't he see she just wanted to keep Aidan safe?

"It's only a shot," she said. "Like a vaccine. He'll hardly notice."

"He'll notice when we have to explain someday we've been tracking his every step."

"It doesn't track steps." Ramona tried to keep her voice even. Phil responded to facts, not feelings. "It only shows position within a few yards, so if something happens, we can find him."

"Ramona, this is nuts. This isn't a police state; it's a perfectly safe neighborhood. The whole reason we moved here was so we wouldn't worry about stuff like that."

He paused and looked away. He knew Ramona was fearful after what happened to Casey. He always said the chances were less than one in a hundred million—that, statistically speaking, this sort of thing would never happen again. It didn't matter to Ramona. She couldn't accept it as random misfortune. To her, it was a message, a sign she must do everything possible to protect her son.

Phil ran a hand through his hair and raised his voice. "They haven't tested the long-term effects of these things. Who knows? It might cause cancer or something."

Ramona snorted. She recognized a cheap scare tactic. "Everything causes cancer."

She looked out the window to the front yard where Aidan played Frisbee with his friend Ryan, the lawn deep green in the mid-June twilight. Ryan tossed the Frisbee—foam, not plastic, after his mother, Whitney, pointed out that a plastic Frisbee could cause jammed fingers and black eyes. Just when Ramona thought she had done everything, Whitney pointed out a gap in her defenses.

Aidan chased the Frisbee across the grass, his body young and smooth. Ramona couldn't imagine it succumbing to the decay of cancer, but she could imagine him getting lost, or—she hardly dared to think the word—taken.

"Ryan," a woman's muffled voice called outside. Whitney appeared on their lawn, come to take Ryan home.

"Whitney's here," Ramona said. She left her dusting and went out the front door, glad for the interruption.

Whitney waved. She wore short denim shorts and a tight green tank-top, dressed more like a teenager than a mom. "These boys," Whitney said. "Come summer, they'd stay out 'til ten if they could."

"I'm sure."

Since the boys had become friends at school, Ramona saw Whitney often. They were the same age, thirty-seven, but Whitney looked older. Her overly tan face bore deep lines. Her mouth had a strange puffy look that made Ramona wonder whether she had gotten a collagen injection.

"Did you talk to Phil?" Whitney asked, voice lowered to a confidential whisper.

"I tried. He hates the idea."

"Too bad. After Doctor Fowler, I feel so much better knowing we can always find him." With Ryan's GPS tracking microchip, his parents could take out their smartphones, pull up a satellite map, and zoom in on a blinking red dot that showed his location in real time. Ramona knew what the app looked like because Whitney had shown her several times.

"Tracy and Andrew had it done with Julia. It's such a relief to have some peace of mind."

"Mm-hm." Peace of mind. Ramona struggled to remember what that felt like. When Aidan was born, she and Phil moved to this suburb where all the families knew each other. There were summer block parties with streets barricaded so kids could safely bike and roller skate. Adults drank Mike's Hard Lemonade out of cans, not bottles, so there wouldn't be any broken glass if one fell. Initially, while other mothers fretted over skinned knees, Ramona aimed for a hands-off approach. When Aidan came whimpering with a cut on his foot, she washed it off in the bathroom, put on a band-aid, and called it done. She hadn't been like them, running to urgent care for every little accident.

Had it only been a year ago? The Bryants lived in the cul-de-sac next to theirs, two photogenic parents with a boy Aiden's age. One day, walking back from a friend's house, Casey vanished. The local news ran a segment with the mother sobbing and begging for information. A witness saw Casey getting into a car that pulled up beside him on the road. He was never found.

"All right, Ryan, let's go," Whitney called. Even with the GPS, she always walked him home, though her place was only five houses down from Ramona and Phil's. "See you, Ramona."

As Ramona watched them leave, she felt the familiar panic, like a small animal scrabbling inside her. Whitney's words needled her, reminding her how simple it might be to protect Aidan—and how easy it would be to lose him. Eight years ago, when Ramona gave up her position as an assistant library director to stay home, she thought she'd go back to work eventually. She hadn't realized then what it would be like. Each new thing Aidan did was a miracle—gelling his hair into little spikes in the front; mixing brownie batter for Phil's birthday, all by himself. She could see only the smallness of his bones, the tender smoothness of his skin. When she tucked him in each night, he looked at her with an unafraid face, with eyes that trusted in her ability to keep him safe.

"Just a tiny pinch," Doctor Fowler pinched Ramona's arm to illustrate, "and he's set for life." The spot on her arm turned red, and she rubbed it. She thought of Phil, away on his business trip. She kept thinking he would pop out from behind a corner, as if his absence were somehow a trap.

Doctor Fowler was a tall man with a toothy grin. Ramona, barely five feet tall, had to look up to catch his gaze. She had never liked tall people for that reason. It seemed to give them an advantage.

"Lucky you, the latest upgrade just came out," Doctor Fowler said. "This one tracks within a square foot. I have it in my dog." He pulled out his tablet and showed Ramona. The satellite map showed an aerial photograph of a suburban house. The red dot raced around in circles in the front yard. He laughed. "She must be pretty bored out there."

"You put it in your dog?" Ramona wasn't sure how that was a selling point.

"Hey, dogs get lost, too. Soon as this one's approved by the FDA, I'm putting it in my kids."

"It's not approved yet?" Ramona wondered if coming here was a mistake.

Doctor Fowler shrugged. "Between you and me, I think the FDA over-regulates. They're just preventing lawsuits against big drug cronies and delaying competing products. In Europe, this thing's already everywhere. Me? I'm holding off 'cause I have a medical license—random audits, you never know. But you? Pay with cash and you were never here."

Ramona looked at Aidan playing on his iPad in the corner. She had given him the large headphones so he wouldn't hear about getting an S-H-O-T. He kicked his legs under the chair. He wore the small, lopsided smile she only saw when he was utterly at ease, unaware she was watching. If this clinic were dangerous, it wouldn't be located in such a new building, with broad glass doors and the reassuring smell of disinfectant. Whitney had given her the names of three other parents who highly recommended Doctor Fowler. His online reviews, though few, were enthusiastic.

"Parent to parent," Doctor Fowler said. "I've had so many people come to me and say how much better they feel after. These days, you can't be too careful."

"No, you can't," Ramona agreed.

"My daughter just learned how to ride a bike." Doctor Fowler showed her a picture on his tablet. A little blond girl teetered on a red bike, glancing nervously at the camera. Her hair fuzzed out from under her helmet, and she wore thick knee and elbow pads. "She didn't want to put those on," he said, pointing, "but I said, 'Damn it, you're wearing them.'"

Ramona smiled, remembering when Aidan first learned to ride. Phil insisted they skip the training wheels, saying they wouldn't teach him anything. Instead, he held onto the back of Aidan's seat and propelled him from behind on roller blades, launching him with a push. When Aidan finally got it, he screamed, "I'm doing it," gaping with joy and panic. Soon, he rode around the street with the other boys, all of them darting back and forth like minnows.

"We all want what's best for our kids. So what do you say? Are you ready for some peace of mind?"

Ramona rested her hand on her purse, touching the lump of her wallet against the fabric. It held eight one-hundred dollar bills. She had withdrawn them from her personal savings account, the one her bitterly-divorced father insisted she keep in her name only for emergencies. She thought about how it would feel: the knowledge that, at any moment, she could check her phone and know exactly where Aidan was. She thought about how Whitney scrubbed Ryan's apples with a special cleaning brush and bought milk from the community farm share down the street. Twice as expensive as regular milk, it was certified free of artificial growth hormones. Whitney could be irritating, but when it came to safety, she was never wrong.

While Doctor Fowler rubbed alcohol with a cotton ball onto Aidan's upper arm, Ramona pressed her son's head to her chest. She stroked his hair and squeezed his palm. When Aidan screeched, Ramona held him tighter, feeling his fluttery breath and his soft skin. She was doing the right thing.

———— ∽∽ ————

When Phil returned from his business trip, he came in the front door lugging his rolling suitcase and a red gift bag. Aidan ran up to him and crashed into his chest.

"How's my boy?" Phil tousled Aidan's hair. "Here, put this in the living room," he said, handing him the bag. "No looking!"

Aidan scurried away, his tiny feet beating a quick rhythm against the floor.

"Ramona." Phil came over to hug her. He squeezed her more tightly than she expected, and she caught his familiar scent: Gillette body wash, an undertone of sweat.

They went into the living room, where Aidan crouched on the braided rug, shaking the bag to guess its contents. Ramona settled into her favorite corner of the couch. Phil, instead of choosing the opposite end, sat close to her. Aidan tore into the bag. He pulled out a Nerf gun, a small orange and blue one resembling a pistol. Aidan grinned. There was a gap in his smile where his left eyetooth had fallen out the week before.

"Wow, Dad, thanks!"

"You got the foam bullets, right?" Ramona whispered. "Not hard plastic?"

Aidan scrambled to his feet, clutching the package. "Can I open it now?"

"You bet," Phil said, "but no Nerf in the house. You know the rules. Let me do that."

Phil took the package and got a Swiss army knife from his pocket. He used a pointed tool to gouge a hole in the corner of the thick plastic. Ramona cringed. She'd seen thick plastic like that slice the hand of the neighbors" boy when he tried to open a toy at his birthday party. Three stitches, Whitney told Ramona later in a censorious tone.

Aidan hovered right near Phil as he flipped open a miniature pair of scissors and cut the hole bigger. Ramona wished Aidan would step away.

"Phil, be careful, it might—"

"Might what?" He wrestled the toy free.

"Never mind."

Aidan snatched the Nerf gun and ran outside, slamming the front door behind him. Ramona expected Phil to follow, but instead, he came over and put his arm around her waist. They went to the window and watched Aidan play.

"That was a nice surprise," Ramona said. "He's been begging for one of those for weeks." Phil stroked the back of her neck. The pressure of his hand soothed her. She leaned back into it and closed her eyes.

"Hey, I'm sorry about the other day," Phil said. "I shouldn't have been so angry. You just want to protect him. You're being a great mom."

"Oh, I just—" Her voice caught in her throat.

"It's weird. When I was a kid, I played at everyone's houses. Got scrapes, fell out of trees, no one cared. But I get why you feel this way. Things are different now."

"I know," Ramona said. She appreciated his nostalgia. She, too, had ridden her bike all over town without fear, buying candy and ice cream at the convenience store. Now it felt like danger lurked in every corner; even the kindest strangers might be kidnappers.

"I'm willing to consider this GPS chip thing," Phil said. "We can do some research, ask around. Who knows? It might be a good idea."

"Oh, Phil, I—" She thought of the money, of the clinic—of how, when leaving, she had glanced out the door to check for anyone she knew. She'd snuck around like an adulterer. She imagined Phil bringing Aidan to Doctor Fowler; Doctor Fowler, bemused, explaining he had already seen this patient.

"What's wrong?" Phil's eyes opened wide. They were blue, like Aidan's. In his concerned face, she saw the Phil she had always known, the one who proposed to her at the top of the Empire State Building, with all the lights of the city sparkling beneath them.

"Nothing. I just love you." She buried her face against his neck so he wouldn't see her guilt.

～～～

"Mom!" Aidan shouted, banging through the front door three days later. "Mom, can I have dinner at Ryan's? He said I could."

Ramona hovered at the stove, managing three pots: spaghetti, red sauce with meatballs, and boiled spinach.

A standard Monday night meal, easy but well-liked by everyone.

Ramona called Whitney. "Hey, Whitney. Aidan says Ryan asked him over for dinner. Is that all right?"

"Absolutely. We're having organic gluten-free veggie burgers over here. Do you want me to come pick him up?" Whitney drove everywhere, even to the bus stop at the entrance of their cul-de-sac. She would run her car with the AC on, chatting to another mom out the open window until Ryan stepped off the bus.

"No, he can take his bike."

"Are you sure?" The gravity in Whitney's voice made it sound like Ramona was sending Aidan on a dangerous journey.

Ramona resisted the impulse to cave. She didn't want to give Whitney the satisfaction.

"I think it'll be fine, thanks." She gave Aidan the thumbs-up sign.

"Bye Mom!" Aidan shouted, scrambling out the door.

"Don't forget to say thank you!" Ramona called after him. She heard the rumble of the garage door as Aidan opened it. She watched him glide down the driveway on his bike.

Since the shot, Ramona felt much more at ease. She checked the app even more than she looked at her email. It was both addicting and reassuring to see Aidan's dot right where he said he would be, whether in Ryan's yard or a friend's house. Sometimes she even checked it while he was at school, comforted at the sight of the dot sitting still in his classroom.

"Just us two for tonight?" Phil said, putting his arms around her from behind.

"Yep."

Phil tickled her, making her splash some sauce on the stove.

"Hey!"

He veered away to set the porch table with the new red and yellow plates, grated Parmesan, and glasses of red wine, not milk, since Aidan wouldn't be there.

Both of them had been more relaxed lately. Ramona suspected her new lack of worry about Aidan pleased Phil. Sometimes, when he looked at her lovingly, she blinked, or pretended she heard her phone buzzing. She could hardly bear the trust in his eyes. She wondered if it looked like she was having an affair. Who would he suspect? Maybe Joe, Whitney's husband. Ramona secretly thought he was good-looking with his strong chin and unruly hair, though she never spoke to him for this reason.

Two hours later, at dusk, they had finished washing the dishes and migrated to the living room. They sat next to each other on the couch. Ramona teased Phil about his three TV remotes while he cruised through channels: a couple kissing, a cowboy riding into the sunset, a woman in high heels stalking a New York City sidewalk. Finally, he gave up, sighed, and put a hand on Ramona's thigh.

Ramona's eyes drifted to the clock. It was nine. "Maybe I should call Whitney." She dialed while sitting on the couch.

Whitney answered after the first ring. "He's leaving now. I was just about to text you. Want me to drive him?"

"No, it's fine. Thanks." A hint of snippiness crept into Ramona's voice. Whitney always acted so high and mighty. She thought she was such a safety guru, when she had no problem injecting botulism and collagen into her own lips.

"He'll be home in a few minutes," Ramona said to Phil. "I'll make sure the light is on."

While Phil started a new Sudoku puzzle from the paper, she went to the front windows to look outside. She puttered around the kitchen, threw out some old newspapers, and wiped down the sink in the bathroom.

She checked her phone. Fifteen minutes had passed. She felt a flutter in her chest. People said to trust your gut instincts, but Ramona's gut had been in overdrive since Casey disappeared, signaling danger at everything.

She finished cleaning the bathroom, taking her time so that each fixture shone. Stashing the Windex under the bathroom sink, she checked her phone again. It was now nine-thirty. She locked the door and turned on the faucet. She pulled up the app. It occurred to her she might be secretly checking like this for years and years.

Hunched over with her elbows on the counter, she looked at the map. It displayed an aerial photo of a house she didn't recognize. Zooming out a little, she saw it was about a mile away from Whitney's, in the opposite direction from her own home. The red dot stayed stationary inside this stranger's house. For a full minute she stared, trying to understand what she was seeing. She called and texted Aidan, but he did not respond.

"Fuck," she whispered. "Shit." She turned off the faucet and exited the bathroom. She opened the side door that led to the porch outside. She tried to move it quietly, but the door made a characteristic squeak.

"Ramona?" Phil called. "Any sign of Aidan?"

"Just a minute," she yelled back.

She stepped outside. The temperature dropped with the sun. Crickets and peep toads screamed in the woods, sounding an alarm. She shut the door and looked up at the menacing stars. Their miserly light emphasized the black, empty the sky and how small she was beneath it.

"Where the fuck is he?" she whispered. She felt an eerie sense of familiarity with this scene. She imagined it so many times, and now it happened. She knew what she had to do.

She held her phone up and dialed 9-1-1, double checking the address of the house: 66 Maple. She paced while it was ringing. She heard the door open behind her. Phil stepped out.

"What's going on?" he asked.

Ramona still had the phone to her ear. It rang three times, and then there was a click.

"Nine-one-one," said a voice at the other end. "What's your emergency?"

"Ramona?" Phil said. She stared at him.

"Hello?" the operator said. "Is someone there?"

"Who's on the phone?" Phil asked.

Ramona hit the End Call button. Her hands shook. She tried to take a deep breath, but the air felt shallow in her lungs. "I think I know where Aidan is. I think we should call the police."

Phil frowned. "How do you know where he is?"

"Phil, I—" She looked down at the phone as though it would tell her what to say.

"You what?" He hated it when she didn't finish her sentences.

"I think I made a big mistake."

She pulled up the app and handed the phone to Phil. He stared at the map, at the red dot sitting stationary in the stranger's house. She waited for him to say something. His mouth hardened into a tense line.

"Ramona." His voice was so low she almost had to lean in to hear it. "I can't believe you did this. Behind my back. When you knew how I felt about it."

"I was desperate." She struggled to maintain control over her voice, which had crept up high and breathless. "I just felt so scared about Aidan after Casey. I shouldn't have done it but I wanted to make—"

"Ramona, what the hell!" Phil shouted, shaking the phone at her. "What is this?"

"Please, Phil, we need to go over there right now." Her voice trembled. "He didn't answer his phone. We need to get in the car."

"All right," he said, nodding sarcastically. "Fine. Not like anything I say will stop you."

Ramona followed him as he stormed back inside and went into the garage. He hit the garage door button with his fist. It fell off the wall and dangled by its wires. As he got into the car, Ramona skittered to the passenger side, desperate to keep up. He turned the key in the ignition and sped down the driveway in reverse. A crunch told her he misjudged on one side, smashing the passenger mirror into a tree.

The wheels screeched as he reversed direction at the end of the driveway and shot down the cul-de-sac. Relief flooded Ramona when she saw no children in the street. In this neighborhood, people drove ten miles an hour at most. Kids thought the cars would always stop for them.

"I think we should call the police," Ramona said, self-conscious of the plaintive note in her voice.

"That's unnecessary," Phil snapped. "He's probably just playing video games at some kid's house."

Ramona's heart fluttered in disagreement, but she said nothing. She rarely admitted it to herself, but sometimes she fantasized about saving Aidan. Her mother's instinct would tell her something was wrong. She would check her phone, see Aidan in some strange location, and fly to the scene. She would pull him from the arms of some jealous kidnapper who had no children of her own.

Phil tore down the dark road, and he turned on the brights. A car approaching from the opposite direction honked as they hurtled past. They flew by the golf course and the town woods, the road too narrow for this speed. Phil swerved when a cat scampered in front of the car, narrowly missing it. Ramona gripped the handle above the window with one hand and her iPhone with the other, staring at the map.

"It's coming up here, on the left," she said. Phil braked hard, and throwing Ramona into her seatbelt. It took her a moment to spot the opening hidden in the trees. He edged the car onto the gravel path, bouncing over potholes. The driveway seemed to be almost mile long.

They came into a clearing that opened onto a lawn, a perfectly trimmed square cut into the woods. In the center of the lawn stood a cement statue of a child with large, blank eyes. The house beyond was small, and a faint blue, flickering light came from a second-floor window.

They got out of the car. Ramona squinted at the house as though that would help her understand why Aidan was inside. She turned to look at Phil, who froze by the open driver's side door. His arms were tense, the muscles defined under his turquoise T-shirt.

"Well," he said. He closed the door of the car, not with his usual joyful slam, but quietly. Ramona trailed behind him as he climbed the stoop and rapped on the front door. No one answered.

Phil knocked again. He crossed his arms and paced across the stoop. Then he pounded with both fists on the door and shouted, "Hey! Open up!"

Almost immediately, Ramona heard the sound of a bolt sliding back. The doorknob turned slowly, so slowly that it almost seemed unreal. Ramona stared as the door opened a crack. In the dim light, she saw a slender woman who appeared to be her age. The woman's hair was tied up in a pony tail and she wore yoga pants.

"Yes?" she said. Her voice was high-pitched and childlike, the doll voice some women affected when they wanted to appear nice.

Phil stepped closer to the door. "Where's my son?" His voice had a slight tremble, and Ramona realized with shock that he was scared.

"Your son? I have no idea what you mean." The woman frowned.

"We know he's here," Phil said. He pushed on the door, but it caught, restrained by a chain lock.

"I don't know what—"

"If you don't let us in now, we're calling the police," Ramona said, surprised at how loud her own voice sounded.

The woman paused. "Well, if you really think he's here, I suppose you can look."

The door closed, followed by a sliding sound as she undid the lock. She opened the door wide to let Ramona and Phil step in. As Ramona's eyes adjusted, she realized the woman couldn't be in her thirties, but actually had gray strands in her hair. Wrinkles showed under her foundation and blush, and her small, tired eyes drooped despite the mascara.

"There isn't much downstairs. Maybe upstairs?" the woman said. She pointed to a staircase on the side of the hall. "Just let me close this." Phil and Ramona moved aside while the woman shut the door and slid a bolt into place. Then she went to the stairs and trudged up them. Phil started after her, but Ramona grabbed his arm.

"Wait," she whispered. She slid the bolt back, unlocking it. She resisted the urge to open the door. Even though she promised herself to always do what was safe, she worried Phil would think opening the door was overkill. It was probably paranoia, her fear that someone else might be lurking in the pale darkness of this house—her sudden wish that she had a pistol, pepper spray, or even a switchblade. When she turned toward the stairs, she saw the woman had paused and turned in their direction, watching.

Ramona stared back at her. If this woman had harmed Aidan, Ramona would slash her face with her car keys. She would stab out her eyes.

"Let's go," she said to Phil. Both of them climbed the stairs. It occurred to Ramona that the house smelled oddly clean, as though bathed in disinfectant. A blue light flickered from the door at the end of the hall, and Ramona caught the woman's silhouette as she walked in.

Ramona rushed after her. Aidan sat on a white leather couch, staring at a large TV in the corner that played a surreal cartoon with strange music. He stirred.

"Mom?" he asked, sounding sleepy.

"Aidan." Ramona strode across the room, took his arm, and tried to get him to stand up. He felt heavier than usual. She pulled on him harder and stared at the woman across the room, who stood motionless and smiling.

"Oh goodness, how could I forget he was up here? He came up my driveway a little while ago. He had lost his phone. I told him he could come inside to use mine. I guess I forgot I let him in."

Phil walked up to her. "Oh, really? Why didn't you call the police?"

"The police? Why?" the woman said, the smile frozen on her face.

Phil leaned over her, threatening. "Do you realize what this looks like, in this day and age?"

"I was only trying to help."

Phil snatched her wrist. "How dare you come near my son."

Ramona grabbed his arm and pulled him back. "Please, Phil, let's just get out of here." The last thing they needed was an assault charge—and something was just wrong in this house, with its emptiness and its sharp clean smell. They had to leave. "Where's his bike?" she demanded.

"I guess it must be out back."

Phil stood by the door while Ramona led Aidan into the hall. All three of them descended the stairs.

"Bye now," the woman called behind them.

Outside, Ramona dragged Aidan into the car. While Phil went around back to grab the bike, she locked the doors, her finger on the button, ready to unlock the second he returned. Upstairs, the woman's shape watched at the window.

When they arrived home, a police car waited outside their house, red and blue lights flashing. An officer stood on the front lawn barking into his walkie-talkie. Neighbors stood whispering in a clump at the edge of the lawn. Whitney was with them, simultaneously chatting with a neighbor and scanning her iPhone, probably for news. Of course Whitney would stand there gossiping instead of texting to ask Ramona if everything was okay.

"Awesome," Phil said. "Just what we need."

Ramona glanced at Aidan in the back seat. He was asleep. She and Phil got out of the car and approached the officer.

"Did one of you call nine-one-one about thirty minutes ago?"

Phil looked away.

"Our son was missing," Ramona said. "I panicked."

"We found him in some woman's house," Phil said. "Someone we don't know."

"Is he all right?" the officer said, frowning.

"Yes, but you should really check this person out," Phil said. "She seemed suspicious." He described what had happened to the officer, who took notes.

"We'll follow up on this," he said.

For the first time that night, Ramona cried. She felt very tired and cold and wanted to be inside with the doors locked, holding a warm cup of tea. To her surprise, Phil wrapped her in a hug.

At first, Aidan claimed the woman had invited him to call home after he lost his phone. Sitting on the living room couch, he shuffled his feet, blushed, and looked at the floor. Ramona realized her son had become a person who could keep secrets, a bigger developmental milestone than crawling or learning to count. Maybe children grew up not in terms of walking, talking, and reading, but in their ability to lie and deceive.

"Is that really what happened?" she asked gravely.

Aidan glanced up at her and squirmed. "I know I shouldn't talk to strangers."

"Aidan, sweetie, you're not in trouble. I just need to know the truth."

"All right..." He drew his legs up onto the couch and laced his arms around them. "She was driving by and saw my Nerf gun. She said it was really cool and she had an even bigger one, if I wanted to see it."

"You were biking home when this happened?"

"Yeah."

Ramona could picture it with appalling clarity: Aidan biking down the side of the road, a vehicle pulling close to him, slowing with the window rolled down.

"Did you get in the car?"

Aidan buried his face in his knees.

"Did you?" She tried to sound gentle.

Without looking at her, Aidan nodded.

"Oh, Aidan," Ramona said. Her voice wavered. "Sweetie, promise me you'll never, ever do that again."

———❀———

Her favorite blazer still fit, the navy one with the sharp collar. So did her khaki pants and the black pumps that gave her a few needed inches. She set her briefcase on the dining room table with a tired thump. It had been an hour and a half drive each way to the city hospital. Her parents' group had met some doctors who were interested in clinical trials of GPS trackers, the beginning of the approval process for FDA's Center for Devices. The doctors sounded receptive, even excited about the possibilities.

Ramona sighed and sank into a chair. Sometimes, she felt her proselytizing wasn't for the doctors' sake as much as for her own. She once had such faith in the GPS. She believed it would allow her, in time of desperation, to swoop in and rescue Aidan. But ever since the encounter at the strange house, she had realized it wasn't enough. What if she looked at her phone and saw Aidan in another town, another state, a place she couldn't reach in time? What if he were in a forest or the middle of the sea? That useless red dot on the map couldn't shield her son's body from the world, from its cruel and roving dangers.

Yet the more she imagined scenarios where the GPS wouldn't help, the more she checked her phone. It was in her hand all the time, nearly every minute of the day. She kept it on the table by her bed. Whenever she woke in the middle of the night, a regular occurrence now, she checked the app.

The police spent several days trying to locate the strange woman, but her house was dark, and no one answered the bell. Neighbors and the local paper both reported that she appeared to have fled. One enterprising reporter discovered no furniture inside, nothing left in the yard; even the statue was gone. Ramona wasn't sure if it was paranoia or her mother's instinct telling her the woman lurked somewhere nearby—a threat that had not disappeared, but simply waited.

Hearing Aidan yelling joyfully outside, Ramona went to the window. He and Ryan were playing in the sprinkler on the front lawn, trying to counteract the summer heat. They jumped up and down in their wet bathing suits. It surprised Ramona that Aidan seemed unshaken. He wanted to play outside as much as usual, puzzled by his parents' worries.

Phil worried now, too. His new fence encircled the front yard. He ordered it the day after they rescued Aidan without asking Ramona about it. He had simply informed her it would cost a few thousand dollars. Ramona didn't dare protest. They had spoken little lately, and what they shared was tense.

Ramona resented that he hadn't asked, and feared what it meant for them, she was glad about the outcome. The fence, constructed of tall wooden planks, blocked the lawn. No one could peer in and see her son—and the only way her son could get out was to come back through the house, a path he knew was monitored by anxious adults.

Ramona glanced down the hall and saw Phil standing in the living room, close to the window, his hands in his pockets, his forehead creased. The window had become his customary place. He stood there whenever Aidan played outside, watching and watching.

FATHOMLESS

Lucy hadn't changed much from what Todd remembered: tangled red curls, blue eyes, pale skin. As she sat down across from him at the table for two, he felt unreal, like his mind had floated out of his body to observe this visitation from his past.

One corner of her mouth went up, the closest she ever got to smiling. "You haven't been too terrible, I hope."

"I suppose I haven't suffered an undue portion of misery," Todd said. Not including, of course, his anguish when she vanished: utter silence for eight months while he grieved and wondered what he had done. Now that he deleted all her emails, she returned: her melancholic voice, her cynical insinuations, her eyes gazing with quiet resignation on something other people couldn't see.

"How's Brahms?" Todd asked.

"Sometimes I wonder why I picked those stupid symphonies. There's nothing left to say. How's your dissertation?" she asked. "Pushed you to consider suicide yet?"

Todd gave a noncommittal shrug. He had forgotten what awful things she liked to say. A guy wearing plaid shuffled past their table, carrying two full mugs to a table where a slender brunette sat waiting, chin in hand.

When he looked back, Lucy lowered her eyes. She wrung her hands under the table, twisting her pale fingers as she always did when deciding whether to lower her shield of pessimism. Did she sense something was wrong? It occurred to him that engagement rings were only for women; it wasn't possible to tell if a man was betrothed.

"I'm sorry for disappearing on you," she said.

Todd did not reply, but looked over at the table where the hipster sat. The brunette had her face buried in her phone. Pained frustration marked the man's face, but he couldn't make her look at him. Todd swallowed. He did it again, but that didn't make the knot in his throat go away.

"Thanks for waiting," Lucy said. "I knew you would."

∿∿

Three years earlier, at the American Musicological Society conference, Todd, then a third-year graduate student, left a lecture on John Cage early. He hadn't been converted by his cohort's zeal for "music" consisting of sneezes, sirens, and barks. He hated timbres created not by instruments, but by the insertion of fish and forks into pianos. Todd, who couldn't even renounce tonality, felt like a church had been defaced. Cage's cold nihilism made his hands clench. Todd climbed over a few pairs of knees to escape, strode out of the auditorium, and burst from the hallway into the chill overcast day.

"Not a fan?" a low voice said. He was unsure of its gender until he saw a young woman about his age sitting on a bench nearby. She leaned forward, her elbows on her knees, wearing a blouse with a feminine necktie, a blazer, slim jeans, and boots. Long red curls flowed down her back, the color of autumn leaves. In one hand she held a cigarette.

She took a puff, expelling the smoke with a thoughtful expression. "I detest Cage." She saw the look on his face and dropped her cigarette to the ground, extinguishing it under her boot. "I only smoke once in a while, for stress." She patted the bench next to her. Usually Todd disliked smokers, but he sensed that her friendliness was only for him, like the sight of a deer in the woods after you sat quiet and still for a long time.

"I'm Lucy."

"Todd."

"Sometimes," Lucy said, "I wonder what ever possessed me to go to graduate school."

Todd gave a short laugh of agreement. "Want to go eat something?"

Together, they ventured out. Near the corner of the hotel, a dead sparrow lay on the sidewalk. Its skull hugged the pavement just a little too flat. The head had twisted around, the wings splayed at a wide angle. One claw stuck up in a final grasp toward the sky, as if the bird had been shocked to find itself on the ground.

"Guess his eye wasn't on that one," Todd said. Lucy laughed.

Over soup and sandwichese, they traded research stories.

"I'm writing about Brahms," she said. "God knows why. Everyone has already said all there is to say on those symphonies."

"Schumann," Todd said. "You think you have this personal connection with a composer. The songs feel like they're yours, until you realize everyone else thinks so too."

Something about Lucy struck him as odd, something in the way she wouldn't smile fully. One corner of her mouth would trip upwards like it wanted to be free, but it couldn't break away from the rest of her somber expression.

"Tell me something about yourself," Todd said. "Something weird."

"All right." Lucy twisted a red curl around her index finger. "When I was a kid, I had this albino rabbit named

Franz. He got away one day and ran into the woods. I cried all night. The next day, I was looking for him in the backyard when I saw something furry in the bushes. It wasn't moving. When I got closer, I saw his head. The coyotes got him."

She paused, looking down at the table, rubbing the handle of her spoon between her thumb and index finger. "The weird part was, I couldn't stop looking at it. It felt like some big secret. I kept thinking, this is what's real. This is what we really are."

Todd's heart quickened. He never thought he would meet someone like himself—someone else with a deep well of darkness, its still, black surface unruffled by everyone else's profligate happiness.

She darted him a glance. "Your turn."

"When I was a kid, my mom's friend brought me this cookie wrapped in aluminum foil to look like a snowman. It was strange, but as soon as I took a bite, I felt terrible. I hadn't realized until then that I really liked the snowman. I had ruined it, and there was no way to make it better again." He looked away as he told her, afraid, but she nodded in understanding.

Todd and Lucy got lunch and dinner together for the rest of the conference. They joked about car accidents, cancer patients, nuclear warfare. They debated over the best way for a musicologist to kill himself if a paper presentation went awry. Lucy advocated jumping off the roof of the hotel. Todd thought drowning was superior.

"You're biased because of your dissertation," she said. Schumann had been committed to an insane asylum after he'd been pulled from the Rhine River by boatmen.

"No, he was simply following neurotic tradition. Ophelia, Die schöne Müllerin. Later on, Woolf."

"Well, I'm still for jumping," Lucy said. "It would be fast. You'd feel like you were flying in your last few seconds."

Todd laughed. "I suppose you have something there."

On the last day of the conference, before Lucy left, he hugged her tightly. She stiffened at first, but then she gave in, and for three entire seconds, she was his. Then she stepped back, turned away, and walked out of the hotel, neglecting to look over her shoulder as Todd hoped. He felt like half of himself had torn away. His insides churned over their own insufficiency.

Both graduate students in their third year, there was no changing their paths. Lucy was at University of Michigan; Todd at Boston University. They sent long emails once every few weeks, detailing in sardonic tones incidents no one else would find funny. He always hoped to see her name in his inbox. He read her words slowly, savoring them. At night, he fantasized about how to seduce her. He would buy her black tulips, chocolate as dark as her soul. He would tell her she was the most exquisitely terrible person he'd ever known.

At the next conference a year later, they arranged to meet at check-in. When she was ten minutes late, he worried her flight had been delayed, or that perhaps her taxi had crashed. But with a turn of the revolving door, she arrived there, in front of him. "Lucy," he said, his voice louder than he'd intended it to be. She gave him a rare smile untarnished by sadness.

They ate lunch and dinner together every day—but other graduate students tagged along, craven networkers. On the first night, trembling, he called her, but she didn't answer. She had been forced to socialize with her cohort. On the second night, Todd had committed to meeting with his advisor. By the final day of the conference, Todd's semblance of sanity was wrecked. If he claimed her now, she would be his—if he failed, he would have to wait several more months.

That afternoon, he skipped the last few talks and took her in a rental car to the arboretum just outside the city.

Lucy opened the passenger window as he drove. Daring to steal glances at her windblown hair, he imagined the trees, waxing red and orange, had turned in imitation of her, their jealousy aroused by her hair.

They walked for hours into the late afternoon, admiring the foamy bark of cork trees, the thorned, spiny ash—which, Lucy said, reminded her of herself. At the top of a hill they sat against the trunk of a maple. The autumn light filtered through the backs of blushing leaves, dousing them in red. He stared at Lucy's fine-boned face, profligate curls, pale fragile hands. She leaned her head against his shoulder. He kissed her ear, her cheekbone, her eyelid, quivering anxiously like his own heart.

That night, they went to her room at the hotel. Todd pressed Lucy against the wall, one hand against the base of her neck, a thumb on the collar bone and the fingers behind—not too hard, afraid of marring her perfect ivory skin. "Lucy," he said, her name the most sensuous syllables he had ever uttered.

Later, when she had fallen asleep, Todd watched her. Moonlight filtered between the beige plastic window slats, striping Lucy and the bed. One stripe illuminated half her face, the curve of one closed eye, the corner of parted lips. Darkness swathed the other half of her face. Todd stored this image on the back of his eyelid, so he could blink it into place whenever he might need it.

In the morning, when Lucy woke up, she sighed. "I haven't packed." She sat on the edge of the bed, wringing her pale hands.

"I'll help you."

"No."

"Breakfast?" Todd asked. She did not reply. He went to Au Bon Pain downstairs and bought back two poppy seed bagels with cream cheese. When he returned, Lucy hadn't moved; she was still sitting on the bed, slumped, staring at the floor. She looked over at him.

"I hate bagels. They make me fat," she said. Streaks marred her cheeks and her voice carried the muffled sound of tears.

"I'll come see you," he said.

"Hope only makes you want what you'll never have."

"I promise."

"I have to go," she said, tears still slipping down her face. Todd wanted to tell her he knew how she felt: rent through with despair on cloudy days, small and solitary under the weight of the universe. But he couldn't bring himself to say it. He watched while she shuffled around the room, stuffing her things into the suitcase. "Bye," she said, her back turned to him. He stood and reached out to touch her, but she turned away.

"Wait."

She stepped into the hall.

Two weeks later, Lucy emailed, apologizing for leaving on such a moody note. Todd told her he didn't mind. They kept in touch as usual. Each time an email arrived, Todd read it over and over until he almost memorized the words. All that mattered was there was someone like him in the world—that, despite the vagaries of geography, he found her.

They arranged for Todd to fly to Michigan in March. Lucy would meet him at the airport. On the plane, Todd's right leg bounced for the entire flight. He turned his grin toward the window, embarrassed by his own elation.

At the baggage claim, he searched the faces, but all of them were strangers. He received no texts or voice messages on his phone. When he called, she didn't answer.

As the hours passed, he lost hope. Had he mistaken the day he was supposed to come? What if she had been killed in an accident, or kidnapped? At a motel near the airport, he searched for her online. The only relevant result was her academic page with a heart-rending profile picture he quickly clicked away from. He called her again; still no answer. It occurred to him that he knew none of her friends and family. They didn't share a single mutual acquaintance. He emailed her academic advisor to ask if she had gone missing. The professor never replied.

Back in Boston, the final draft of his dissertation languished, unedited on his laptop. He couldn't bear to think about Brahms, the composer whose love for Clara Schumann had never been returned. He slept sixteen hours a day and stopped doing laundry. His advisor frowned at him, but he couldn't make himself care.

Some months later, Todd sat at a table in the student center, trying to read an article on Chopin's piano sonatas. His advisor made it clear he needed to take teaching more seriously, or his funding would be at risk. There wasn't much to lose, but Todd couldn't afford even a small financial blow. As usual, he'd wasted most of his worthless day. He woke at ten, dragged himself out of bed an hour later, and ate a few crackers for lunch. Now he struggled to work in this obnoxious place, as if the noise and brightness might jump-start him. So far, it had only given him a headache.

"I'm sorry, but can you help me?" someone asked.

Todd lifted his head, and a girl smiled back at him. Her bright outfit struck his eyes like an interrogation light: an emerald sweater, purple jeans, gold shoes. Her hair hung around her shoulders in long, blonde waves. Todd couldn't remember the last time he'd seen anything so colorful.

"Do you know where Carr Hall is?"

"That building." He gestured with his head. "Second floor."

"Thanks," the girl said, but she didn't leave. "Are you reading about Chopin? I love him!" Uninvited, she sat down. "Are you a musician?"

"Graduate student. Musicology, not performance."

"Cool. I used to play piano. I'm Brittany, by the way."

He didn't want to reply, but her expectant look made him feel guilty. "Todd," he said.

"Kind of random, but I have tickets to the symphony this weekend. Friend of mine was supposed to go, but she flaked out. Want to come? They're playing Beethoven's Violin Concerto and Shosty Ten."

"Shosty," the nickname musicians used for Shostakovich, marking Brittany as one of those with experience, who might actually have ears in this deaf world. Shostakovich's Tenth was one of Todd's favorite symphonies. Beneath layers and layers of resignation, he felt the stirring of vague interest.

"Sure," he said. "Why not."

It had been a long time since Todd had attended an actual concert. Graduate school, intended to be his apotheosis into a lifetime of art, revealed itself as drudgery: shuffling through mildewed library stacks, grading papers, informing apathetic undergrads of the differences between Mozart and Tchaikovsky. He relaxed into his seat, letting the sound buoy him, remembering what it was like to listen to music and feel moved by it. At intermission, he found himself talking about how Brahms had been in love with Schumann's wife. No one knew exactly what happened during Schumann's stint at the asylum and eventual death, but Todd believed Brahms had been rejected.

"That's so tragic!" Brittany said. "Life shouldn't be that way."

Brittany told Todd she was a medical student. "I do some research in addition to my classes. Right now, I'm working on pancreatic reprogramming. Basically, trying to convert one specialized cell type into another. It might lead to a cure for diabetes."

"Wow," Todd said. "That makes me feel useful."

"Oh, come on. What would be the point of curing diabetes if we didn't have things like music?"

Todd blinked a few times, squinting. It was the best thing he had heard in a while.

Brittany instituted a program of experiencing all the musical groups in Boston. They went to the Boston Baroque, Handel and Hadyn, the early music festival, and various chamber groups. "I don't get nearly enough arts with my medical studies," she said, resting her hand on his arm. "I'm starved."

The thought of being happy frightened Todd. But sometimes, he found himself smiling along with Brittany, and anticipating when he would see her next, his sadness confined into a smaller and smaller space, until it evaporated altogether. He focused on finishing his dissertation and preparing for his thesis defense. The theme of Brahms' Third Symphony comes from measure 201 of Schumann's Third Symphony, Todd typed. The interval of a sixth, prominently featured in both symphonies, marks Brahms as a man indebted to and defined by Schumann.

It was restaurant week, and Brittany picked out an Italian place they couldn't otherwise afford. He looked forward to ordering shrimp scampi, or lobster ravioli, maybe some Caprese salad on the side.

Now that happiness had crept back into his life, Todd wondered why he had been so bent on suffering. He closed his laptop and his scores. It was time to pack his things for spending the night at Brittany's.

After ten months, while they sat on the futon at her apartment, she ambushed him. "You're graduating soon, and so am I." She nestled her head on his shoulder. Her hair smelled good: something fresh and maybe something flowery. "I don't want this to end. I want to stay with you."

Todd wanted to hit himself with something, or throw his mug at the wall. He shouldn't have given up. He should have done something, anything, other than fly back home and forget. He knew she suffered from melancholy, so why hadn't he surmised hers might be worse than his?

If he had the courage to reach out and brush the back of her hand with tentative fingers, she would look at him with eyes wide and unsecretive, giving him the strength to cover her entire hand with his. He could still do it—he could still, so easily, throw everything away.

Todd grabbed the edge of the table to stop everything from shattering. "Lucy," he said. "I— I think I—" She looked up, lips slightly parted, daring to hope.

"Todd!" said a cheerful voice at the door. Brittany flounced over, eyes shining. Her smile was as white as piano keys. Lucy studied her, baffled that Todd would associate with such a person.

The words rushed out before Todd had decided to say them. "This is Brittany—my fiancée."

"Great to meet you!" Brittany stuck out an eager hand. Lucy stared at it like an insult. She glared at Todd with narrowed eyes. Brittany shrugged and pulled an empty chair close to Todd's, kissing him on the cheek.

"Todd said you were at Michigan," Brittany said. "How do you like Ann Arbor?"

"I have to go," Lucy said. "I have to meet a friend." She grabbed her purse from under the chair and stood. Todd wanted to say goodbye, but couldn't make a sound.

When Todd was thirteen, his father bought him a model sailboat. The box arrived as a surprise in the mail. Inside were the instructions, the parts shielded in bubble wrap. Todd spent two hours assembling it with his father. The cobalt hull shone. The mainsail and the jib almost glowed, crisp and white, with tiny ropes woven of coarse thread. Todd set the boat on a stand in the corner of his room. On nights when the moon poured in through his window, he left his curtains open and pretended his room was the fathomless ocean, his boat the only thing for miles around, drifting through untarnished moonlight on a still, shining sea.

It was too good for him, just like his father. Todd's love for him somehow hurt. He made grilled cheese every Sunday afternoon, browning the bread to a precise degree and transporting the sandwich to Todd's plate with a masterful flick of the spatula. In the mornings, he came downstairs with his shoes untied and his shirt untucked, grinning as Todd's mother came over and kissed him.

Every day, his father said they would take the boat out, but fortunately, things had gotten in the way. Todd knew once the boat set sail, it would never be as perfect as it was now.

One Saturday, when his father and mother had gone to lunch with friends, Todd carried the boat to the lake. Using the remote control, he drove it as far away as possible and then turned the switch off. The wind blew toward the opposite shore; the boat shrank to a half its size, then an eighth. Once it was a tiny white spot Todd turned his back to it.

He told himself he had only met the inevitable sooner. But he made a mistake and wished he could rewind time and have the boat back in his hands. He should have kept it until it fell apart.

Todd watched Lucy through the window. She walked head down, hands in her pockets, drifting around the people in her way, who went straight at her like she didn't exist. It was up to her to change, like a leaf in a stream rushing around the rocks in its path. How could they not see her? She was the most beautiful and unnoticed person in the world.

When Lucy escaped the view offered by the window, Todd knew better than to press his face against the glass for one last half-second glance.

"She seemed odd," Brittany said.

"She's a bit of a loner." In this new language he had learned, loner meant all the bad things a person could be—antisocial, weird, peculiar, sad.

"Huh," Brittany said, brow furrowed over this mystery. "I guess you can't force people to be happy."

"No," Todd said. "I guess you really can't."

PEANUT BUTTER

There were four ways to kill someone with peanut butter, and Beth had listed them herself. So it was practically her own fault, Anna reasoned, that the last way was so easy.

Gym was the best time, when she had easy access to Beth's lunchbox. In the midst of the dodgeball melee, Anna frowned, rubbed her stomach, and muttered to the male gym teacher about a certain time of month, earning a blush and unlimited bathroom rights. On her way to the lockers, she paused to watch Beth run from a boy who slung ruthless dodgeballs at the weak. Beth escaped him, but she wouldn't escape this.

Anna crept into the changing room and opened the locker she shared with Beth. She opened Beth's backpack, unzipped her lunchbox, and took out one of the two hummus sandwiches, tossing it into the trash. She replaced it with the decoy from her own lunchbox. She'd made it to look just like Beth's: wheat bread, hummus smeared around the edges to disguise the peanut butter, neatly folded plastic wrap. She shoved the sandwich into Beth's lunchbox and zipped up the backpack. She slammed the locker shut and left.

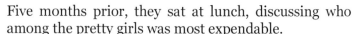

Five months prior, they sat at lunch, discussing who among the pretty girls was most expendable.

"Alyssa thinks the fate of the universe depends on her hair," Jamie said. "She just spent, like, twenty minutes fixing it in the bathroom."

"Sophia's practically illiterate." Anna scoffed and rolled her eyes. "She says The Hatchet is too hard."

"I came up with a new list," Beth said. "Four ways to kill someone with peanut butter. One: Stuff it in their nose and mouth, asphyxiate them. Two: Buy it in a glass jar, bash them over the head. Three: Lace it with arsenic, offer them a bite."

"What's the fourth way?" Jamie asked.

"Use it on someone with a peanut allergy. Like me."

Anna and Jamie sat in silence, unsure whether to be amused or concerned. They always spent lunchtime disparaging normal girls, or "clones," but Beth's recent outbursts had turned violent. Two weeks into eighth grade, and already she invented several lists for unlikely murder weapons, including microwaves and spoons.

"Look, another sheep joining the herd," Jamie said. At the next table, a new girl, led by Sophia, sat to squealed greetings. A moment later, she was indistinguishable from the others.

"Speaking of clones," Beth said, "Anna, what are you wearing?"

"My mom got them," Anna said, denouncing the skinny jeans she had secretly chosen herself.

"Tell your mom not to buy you such sexist clothes. They make you look like them!"

"Is that such a bad thing?" Anna had grown tired of hiding inside baggy sweatshirts and behind glasses. At home, she took off her thick frames in front of the mirror and examined her face. Logically speaking, she looked no worse than other girls. If she got contacts and smoothed her hair, she might appear normal, perhaps even attractive—but that would betray her friends, who strove so valiantly not to be like everyone else.

"Yes, it's a bad thing!" Beth said. "Do you want to be objectified?"

A retort rose in Anna's throat. Just because Beth wanted to dress like a hobo didn't mean Anna had to. But before she could defend herself, the bell rang, and the girls scurried to science class.

Beth had always been dictatorial. Once, when Jamie wore a hot pink shirt to school, Beth said, "You look like Barbie." Jamie never wore the shirt again. Afterwards, Beth went vegetarian, and no one could eat meat for lunch. She said Anna's ham sandwich smelled like dead animal, and ever since then, Anna brought plain cheese to school.

<hr />

She revealed Anna's punishment for wearing skinny jeans in science, when Miss Bennett announced it was time to pick lab partners for the year. As the selection process erupted, chairs scraping and students scrambling, Anna looked at Beth. Their friendship survived other conflicts in the past—a history class rivalry in fifth grade, a battle over robotics team strategy in seventh. But instead of returning Anna's gaze, Beth looked down.

"Jamie and I are partners," Beth said. "We decided this morning."

Annoyed, Anna stared at the remainders. Everyone already stood next to best friends and crushes, leaving only three to mill in uncertainty. One was the girl with raccoon makeup and black fingernails. One was the boy who once told Anna she looked like a witch because she had a pimple on her nose. The last was the new girl: the latest sheep in the herd.

The new girl wore skinny jeans and a pink chiffon top and had her hair in a high, sleek ponytail. She caught Anna's eye and smiled. Beth would judge. Beth would complain. But now that Anna thought of it, she didn't know why she allowed Beth to boss her around in the first place. There was no reason to obey her anymore.

"Want to be partners?" Anna asked.

"Sure," she replied. "I'm Krysta."

They retreived three test tubes from Miss Bennett's desk, each containing a mystery solution. They had to identify the elements using a flame test. Anna expected Krysta to ask for help, but she turned on the Bunsen burner with practiced ease.

"The school website mentioned a robotics club," Krysta said, holding the test tube over the flame with tongs. "Do you know anything about it?"

"Yeah, my friends and I are in it. We do the FIRST challenge."

"Really?" Krysta asked, eyes wide. "We did FIRST at my old school! Can I join?"

Her enthusiasm surprised Anna. "Sure, why not?"

Overnight, Krysta's judgment somehow superseded Beth's in importance, and Anna decided to wear her skinny jeans for the second day in a row. The next day, she led Krysta to the lunch table like an exotic wild beast.

"This is Krysta," Anna said. "She wants to join robotics."

Beth stared. Miss Bennett's robotics team was the domain of her three-girl clique; forbidden, in the off chance they might want to join, to all clones. Last year, Beth declared it a feminist robotics club, so even nerdy boys met with great reluctance—and when Miss Bennett wasn't watching, made to feel their inferiority through forced counting of Lego kits.

"I saw you with Sophia yesterday," Beth said. "Sure you want to sit with us?"

Anna glared at her, but Krysta didn't seem to mind. "Sophia wasn't my type," she said. "But maybe you are."

Beth rolled her eyes, then turned her attention to her second sandwich, which she wolfed as hungrily as the first. She brought two sandwiches to lunch each day, always with unusual combinations: hummus and cucumber, banana and fluff, Swiss and grape jelly.

"You'll have to get Miss Bennett's permission. It's her club. She's done stem cell research, at Harvard." Beth stared at Krysta, as though expecting her to be intimidated.

"Really? That's amazing!"

Beth shrugged, and to Anna's surprise, stopped trying to dissuade her.

In her first robotics meeting that afternoon, Krysta discovered using a color sensor helped the robot bring "groceries" back to base, a task that had stumped the team for some time. As Anna watched, she felt a warm swell of admiration. "How'd you do that?"

"I built off Beth's idea, using the light sensor for the fishing task." Krysta smiled at Beth. Instead of making a sarcastic remark, Beth pursed her lips and looked away.

"She's actually okay," Beth admitted later, while she and Anna waited outside for Anna's mother to pick them up. For Krysta to have been pronounced "okay," despite using mascara, wearing skinny jeans, and carrying a pink purse, was unprecedented. Anna grinned, feeling as though Krysta's victory over Beth's edicts was her own.

In October, Miss Bennett announced a new project: Adaptation Island. Each pair of lab partners would combine two animals to invent an imaginary creature. They would research animal behavior and write weekly about how the animal adapted to natural disasters. To Anna's delight, Krysta invited her to work on it at her house after school. The next day, she followed Krysta to her bus, gripping the pink bus pass like the key to a forbidden castle.

Krysta's room had a queen-sized bed draped with a chiffon canopy and book shelves stuffed double with glossy science books. A poster of the Andromeda galaxy hung on one wall—and on the floor, a pair of twisted purple panties lay in a heap.

"Oh God, that's embarrassing." Krysta scooped them up and stuffed them under her bed, turning red all the way to her ears.

Discovering a shared interest in entomology, they invented a creature called the "flant," a combination of a butterfly and an ant. They finished by four o' clock, but Anna's mother wasn't coming to pick her up until five thirty. After they played a game of checkers, Krysta reached across the board and took Anna's glasses off. Anna blinked. Usually, she hated when other people touched her glasses, but Krysta's gesture didn't bother her.

"You're really pretty without glasses," Krysta said. "Have you ever worn makeup?"

Anna shook her head, feeling her cheeks grow hot.

"I bet some mascara would really bring out your eyes."

Anna tried to hold steady while Krysta brushed mascara on her lashes. She took out a tube of pink lip gloss, smeared some onto an index finger, and brushed it across Anna's lips. The light pressure of her fingertip was pleasant and smooth. It tasted like strawberry.

~~~

Each week, Anna and Krysta researched the habits of butterflies and ants. They documented flant migratory patterns after a volcanic explosion and reported how it preyed on other creatures in famines. In the spare time before Anna's mom came, Krysta taught Anna how to use makeup. She styled her hair and let her try on clothes. One week, she said, "Let's play dress-up." She opened her closet at one end, revealing colorful party dresses, and started to change right in front of Anna. Anna watched as she flung her shirt off, then blushed and stared at the floor, wondering why she hadn't looked away in the first place.

"Done." Krysta posed. The one-shoulder emerald dress looked awfully revealing, showing her entire shoulder and graceful arm.

"Try this." She shoved a bundle of fabric toward Anna. Anna fumbled with the button of her jeans, feeling nervous even though Krysta had turned away. There was no way she'd ever look as perfect as Krysta did—tan and sleek, almost air-brushed. Adolescence left Anna skinny in all the wrong places, arms and legs jutting out awkwardly like they weren't really hers. She took off her clothes and pulled the white dress down over her head, shifting it into place. It actually fit well. She held out the glittering tulle skirt as she turned back and forth in front of the mirror.

"You look adorable!" Krysta grabbed Anna's hands and spun her around. "Now you need accessories. You can borrow anything you want."

Anna ran her fingers through the necklaces dangling from pegs on the wall, admiring pearls and silver chains. She choose one with a golden starfish charm. "What about this?"

Krysta frowned. "That was my grandma's. I don't want anything to happen to it, you know?" Embarrassed, Anna let go. She was relieved when Krysta changed topics by holding up earrings to either side of her face.

Anna shook her head. "My ears aren't pierced." She told Krysta how Beth thought it was ridiculous to punch holes in your body for hanging decorations, especially since boys didn't have to.

Krysta laughed. "Beth would say that. There's nothing wrong with being pretty, but I like how she's not afraid to be different."

"You're a lot more different than she is. She dresses to show her personality, just like everyone else. You don't care about that. You're unpredictable." Anna paused and looked away. "I think that's really cool."

Krysta tilted her head. Her earrings glittered against her hair as they fell sideways. "Really? Aw, thanks." She held out her arms. "Give me a hug?"

She wrapped her arms around Anna and pressed close against her. The scent of something flowery made Anna feel dizzy and warm. She had always liked boys, but for some reason, the desire to kiss Krysta flitted through her mind.

"Who wants to go on a field trip?" Miss Bennett waved a stack of flyers in the air. Anna snatched one. In bright red and blue type, it advertised a weekend FIRST conference in Boston. Students from participating schools could meet NASA engineers who built real robots.

When Anna and Krysta sat down to complete their PowerPoint on world food supply for the presentation segment of the competition, they hunched close together.

"Look, this says we'll be staying in the Park Plaza Hotel," Krysta whispered. "It's an overnight field trip."

"It would be our first ever," Anna said, pressing her leg briefly against Krysta's. She thought of last week when Krysta, whispering into her ear, had accidentally licked it.

"Do you think Beth will be able to go?"

Anna frowned, unsure why Krysta would ask that. A moment later, a crash and a shriek rang from the other side of the room, where Jamie and Beth had been doing practice runs with the robot.

"Oh no! Krysta!" Beth's voice was desperate and high-pitched. "I broke the attachment you built!" Anna and Krysta rushed over. The robotic arm Krysta made for bringing in the groceries lay shattered on the floor. The rest of the robot remained suspiciously intact. Anna crossed her arms and stared at Beth, who loved to fabricate drama in order to get attention.

Krysta swooped down to pick up the pieces. "Oh, oh, don't worry, it'll be easy to fix," she said.

"I ruined it!" Beth wailed.

"No you didn't, not at all." Dropping the Legos on the table, Krysta hugged Beth.

It took Anna a moment to figure out why she felt so stung: She thought she was the only one who had gotten a hug from Krysta.

At home, Anna shoved the permission slip at her mother, who frowned as she read it.

"That's when your grandmother is visiting."

Anna's heart sank. "But I'll see her at Christmas!" she whined.

"She's getting older, and she wants to see you." Nothing could change her mother's mind, not even promising to do all the chores in the house for a week.

Anna relayed the terrible news while they stood by their lockers, hoping Krysta would be as heartbroken as she was. At the very least, she might get a hug out of it. But Krysta just frowned and said, "That really sucks. I'll tell you all about it when I'm back."

The minute the school bus was scheduled to leave—8:35 on Saturday morning—Anna scrolled through all of Krysta's Instagram pictures. Most were close-ups, solemn-eyed shots Krysta had taken herself. Anna reached out to touch her computer screen, but it felt nothing like Krysta's face.

All weekend, she moped in her bedroom, checking each time her phone pinged with an Instagram update.

Beth updated regularly. None of the photos contained Jamie—only Beth and Krysta. There was a picture of her and Krysta hugging. One shot showed them smiling over a plate of spaghetti in a restaurant, grinning cheek to cheek. In another photo, they both held a small robot, hands touching.

Anna tried to reassure herself. Beth hadn't tried on dresses at Krysta's house, or worn her makeup and jewelry. Krysta was probably just being nice to her because she was good at robotics. Anna texted Krysta repeatedly, but she never replied.

That Monday at the lockers, Krysta smiled and hugged Anna.

"I missed you!" she said. Anna felt warm with happiness.

But later in the bathroom, Beth wore a smug, cold smile. "We met engineers from NASA. One of them told me I should consider MIT." She smoothed her hair in the mirror, a gesture Anna had never seen before. She wore a necklace with a starfish charm. Beth never wore jewelry, but the pendant looked familiar.

"That necklace," Anna said, pointing.

"Yeah. It was Krysta's grandma's, but she let me borrow it. She trusts me."

Anna frowned and crossed her arms, hoping Beth was lying. "I knew her first."

"So?"

"So, I know her better. She's my friend." Beth needed to understand that Krysta was Anna's friend, her property, possibly even more.

"Yeah. Friend. And that's what you'll always be."

Anna smacked the sink. "What does that even mean?" She had the feeling she was about to discover something she already suspected, sensed in moments when Krysta didn't respond to her texts, or mysteriously couldn't hang out because of other commitments.

Beth smiled and whispered, leaning forward so that the starfish charm dangled out from her chest. "We kissed."

"You're lying!" Anna said.

Beth took out her iPhone and showed her a picture: Beth grinning into the camera while Krysta kissed her on the cheek.

"That doesn't count."

"Oh yeah?" Beth scrolled through a few more pictures, Beth and Krysta cheek-to-cheek, Beth and Krysta actually kissing, on the lips. "You can be Krysta's friend. But you'll never know her like I do."

"You—" Anna knew what she wanted to say, but she had never said it out loud before. "You bitch," she muttered.

"What was that?" Beth said, holding her hand to her ear.

Anna stormed out of the bathroom, banging the door against the wall outside.

<hr />

The rest of the day, she fumed at her desk, thinking about what she'd like to do to Beth. She could sneak up behind her at lockers and grab her hair. She could steal the periodic table from inside her locker, rip it up, and stuff the pieces back inside. But then she got a better idea.

Back in elementary school, Beth had accidentally eaten a candy bar with peanuts. Her face turned red, she wheezed, she cried. It would serve justice to turn one of Beth's own revenge schemes on her. She deserved it: to feel how Anna felt, to have this knot in her throat, to be on the edge of crying.

That night at home, Anna took two slices of wheat bread from her parents' loaf on top of the refrigerator. She grabbed the jar of peanut butter from the cabinet and spread a generous layer on each slice of bread, keeping the peanut butter away from the edges so it wouldn't show. She filled the outer part of the bread with hummus, so it would look like Beth's. Anna then took out a swath of plastic wrap and folded it tightly around the sandwich, just like Beth did. This would teach Beth right.

—————∼∼∼—————

After gym ended, and everyone else rushed to the cafeteria for lunch, Anna ducked into the bathroom and hid, terrified of what might happen at the lunch table. What if Beth had already eaten the sandwich? Would Anna hear screaming? Would someone know to look for the EpiPen Beth carried in her library volunteer tote bag? The worst possibility crept into Anna's mind: what if Beth died? Beth's allergy wasn't fatal—but now that she thought of it, she'd heard peanut allergies could suddenly worsen without warning. People died like that all the time.

If Beth did die, would they be able to trace the origin of the sandwich? Would Anna go to juvenile hall, with all the delinquent boys? She could barely breathe. She considered staying in the bathroom for the entirety of lunch, but couldn't bear the uncertainty. If Beth chose the safe sandwich first, there still might be time to stop her.

Anna strode into the cafeteria and discovered Jamie sitting quietly, alone.

"There you are," Jamie said. "I thought I'd have to eat all by myself."

"Where are Beth and Krysta?" Anna asked, afraid she'd missed it all.

"In Miss Richard's room. They wanted to talk about starting a book club or something."

An ambulance came wailing into the parking lot. Students squealed and flocked to the front window, which was soon blocked by the growing herd. Anna and

Jamie rushed to join them, but Anna could see nothing. She jumped up and down, trying to catch a glimpse over the heads of her classmates. She saw pieces in slow motion: the principal, the teachers, EMTs wheeling someone in a stretcher.

Hysteria rose in her throat. "Oh my god!" She caught a glimpse of the person on the stretcher but couldn't tell who it was. She jumped again. An EMT blocked the view.

Someone tapped her on the shoulder. She spun so fast that the person took a step back. It was Beth.

"Oh my God!" Beth wailed. "Krysta!"

Anna stared at her, unable to understand what was happening. "Where is she?"

"She ate my sandwich."

"What?"

"She forgot her lunch, so I gave her one of mine," Beth sobbed. "She started getting all red and choking."

"So the ambulance—"

"It was peanut butter. She's allergic. I have no idea how it got there."

The enormity of what she had done hit Anna like a dodgeball to the stomach. That the sandwich might fall into someone else's hands—someone with a peanut allergy, someone she'd never hurt in a thousand years— had never occurred to her.

Meanwhile, Beth cried as vehemently as she gave her righteous speeches, in great gulps and sobs until she was red in the face. The sight of Beth tear-ridden and broken terrified her somehow, and Anna felt the urge to hug her. But she decided not to be the first to make a move. It would be up to Beth to change things, to undo the damage.

Beth took a step toward Anna. Then she paused, turned, and hugged Jamie instead.

Within a few days, Krysta reappeared in homeroom, pale but well-dressed as usual, wearing an almost-sheer black chiffon top that showed glimpses of her bra. While Beth and Jamie rushed desperately toward her, Anna hardly knew what to say. She avoided Krysta for a week. Then, one day, she ran into her in the bathroom.

"Anna," Krysta said. "I'm so glad you're here. We need to talk." She glanced under the stalls to see if anyone else was there.

Anna stared at her feet, scared that Krysta knew. "About what?"

"Beth," Krysta whispered. "I'm scared. What if she did it on purpose?"

"Wait. You mean the sandwich?"

"Yeah."

Anna paused, trying to wrap her mind around this new development. "Why would she do something like that?"

"We were—well, we were kind of dating, a little." Krysta looked at her as though to judge her reaction. Anna nodded, keeping her expression neutral. "It was nothing serious, at least for me. But Beth was getting all intense about it. She hated that I was hanging out with you so much. One day, I told her to stop being so possessive, and she got really mad."

"So you think she might have done it on purpose? Like, for revenge?"

"Yeah. You hear these stories about controlling people. You know, 'If I can't have you, no one can.'" Krysta's eyes were wide and beautiful, filled with trust. "Do you think I should tell someone?"

"You're telling me," Anna said. She could hardly believe her good fortune—that suddenly, Beth was dangerous, while she, Anna, was the harbor to which Krysta returned.

The bell rang, and they moved toward the door. They reached for the handle at the same moment, brushing hands.

"Why don't you come to my house today?" Krysta said. "We can talk more there."

"Definitely."

Anna held the door open and let Krysta go first. As she admired Krysta's graceful walk, swinging ponytail, and tiny purse, she felt a surge of pride. Everything had turned out so wonderfully, so well.

THE GRECHTZOAR

"We'll need weapons," Carl said. They stood in Jimmy's garage, surrounded by bags of potting soil and gardening tools. Carl hefted a small shovel. "Think you can handle this?"

Jimmy nodded and took it, lifting it nervously to see if he could swing it against an attacker. Though only half his height, it was heavy, with a thick, sharp blade.

"I'll take these," Carl said. He picked up a pair of long garden shears. "Okay, here's the plan." He opened his backpack to show Jimmy the contents: a folded blue tarp, a package of raw beef, and rope. "We'll follow its tracks into the woods. When we find its lair, we'll climb a tree nearby. I'll throw the beef down, and when it's eating, I'll throw the tarp down on it. Then we'll tie it up."

Jimmy kept hoping his mom would call them in for lunch or that his phone would ring and he'd have to answer it.

"What if it attacks us?" he asked.

"If it attacks one of us, the other will fight it off." Carl pretended to snap his garden shears at a vicious beast. "Take that! And that!" He laughed.

Jimmy imagined what they would look like to a monster sneaking up from behind: two vulnerable backs, laughably armed in the wrong direction. Short twelve-year-old legs that couldn't run fast enough, no matter how hard they tried.

"Hey Carl? Maybe this isn't such a good—"

"Come on, Jimmy, man up," Carl said, grinning and slapping him on the back. "It's your chance to prove you're not a chicken, remember?"

It started last night when Jimmy went out on the porch to get the spare key from under his doormat. It had been part of his bedtime routine ever since a boy his age had disappeared two months ago. No one knew exactly what happened. Some people said he'd run away, while others whispered that he'd been taken from inside his own home, and would never be seen again.

Jimmy couldn't stop thinking about the second one. In school, he kept sneaking glances at the empty desk in the corner, the whispered words echoing in his mind. Disappeared, taken—kidnapped. They made him feel keenly aware of his smallness, four and a half feet tall and skinny as a stick. At home, a kidnapper could hide almost anywhere in his room: under the bed, behind the bureau, inside the closet. He hated opening the front door at night, but if he didn't take the key in, he'd wake up later, his sweaty sheets tangled around his knees.

He stepped out with his trembling flashlight and knelt, keeping his head up to watch the edge of the woods across the street. Jimmy swept the faint white circle of light across the bushes, the last line of defense between his house and total wilderness. Usually everything was dark, but he thought he saw something shine. His breath caught in his throat, as though an invisible hand had squeezed his lungs. Slowly, he moved the flashlight back.

Then he saw it: two reflective circles, like eyes. The circles stayed for a second, as though staring at him. Then, in an instant, they disappeared. He thought he saw the bushes rustling.

Jimmy gasped. He'd practiced dashing inside lots

of times, slamming the door and locking the bolt, for a moment just like this. But now he couldn't move. He noticed something at the foot of the bush. It was his baseball glove. The boy next door had thrown it into the bushes after snatching it from him earlier that day. After running inside to sniffle and eat a comfort popsicle, Jimmy had completely forgotten to retrieve it.

He ran inside and slammed the door. Jimmy's hands shook as he slid the key into the bolt. The clicking sound reassured him—its reassurance that a thick piece of metal stood between him and any attacker. He grabbed the three empty coffee cans he left by the door and hurriedly stacked them in front, so anyone breaking in would wake him up. His trembling fingers dropped them, and they clattered on the tile. Swallowing hard, Jimmy stacked them again before scrambling into the living room.

His mother sat in one of the reclining chairs, reading a book. "Jimmy?" she said, looking at him. "Everything all right?"

"Yeah." He knew better than to tell her. She was the one who made him put the key back out every morning. She said it was a safe neighborhood with nothing to be afraid of. Everyone seemed to have forgotten about the boy who vanished.

He ran upstairs to his room and claimed his copy of *Flaherty's Handbook of Mystical Creatures* from under the bed. A page in the back gave directions for reporting a sighting:

To Report A Sighting
If you have spotted a mystical creature, call Herb Flaherty, Editor, at 555-920-4567. Provide the name of the creature, time seen, and location. Your sighting may be included in the next edition of Flaherty's Handbook.

Jimmy flipped through the handbook, looking for the right entry. Some part of him knew exactly what the thing in the bushes was. It had bulging white eyes; it was about his height; it must've had black fur, since it blended in with the dark. Now that he thought about it, there had been a lump sticking out of the bush. That must have been its snout. There were twenty creatures in the book, most of them harmless: pixies, nymphs, unicorns. But there was something malevolent about the thing Jimmy had seen. It had to be a *grechtzoar*.

Fumbling with his phone, he called Carl. While the phone rang, Jimmy scanned the grechtzoar's page. The handbook described it as a large black animal like a dog with sharp claws and teeth stained pink with the blood of its prey. Worst of all were the eyes, white and opaque like crystallized clouds of fog. Grechtzoars were almost blind, but they had an excellent sense of smell. If a grechtzoar liked your scent, it became obsessed. It would hide, it would lurk, it would stalk, until finally it caught you, satisfying its lust.

"What up?" Carl said, finally answering.

"Get out your handbook. I saw it." He didn't want to say the actual name, as though pronouncing it might conjure up the monster in his room.

"The grechtzoar? No way! You report it?"

"Not yet." Jimmy felt queasy. He wasn't sure what it had been doing near his house, but it couldn't have been good. "I thought maybe you could do it."

"I ripped out the page with the number, but I don't know where I put it. Hey, are you thinking what I'm thinking?"

The boy had never been found. At school, kids talked around him in whispers, never calling him by name.

"The grechtzoar must've got him," Jimmy said.

"Exactly. We'll have to track it."

"Wait, are you crazy?"

"We can't just let it terrorize our neighborhood. It could be munching on someone's baby right now. It's up to us to catch it. We'll be heroes!"

"But that thing was practically the size of me. It could bite your head off."

Carl sighed. "You're not chicken, are you? You know everyone says you are because of the poodle."

Last year, after reading a news story about rabies, Jimmy had run screaming from a woman's poodle at recess. It acted a little too excited, and he thought he'd seen foam in its mouth. Once the story spread around school, his reputation was destroyed.

"It's your chance to prove them wrong," Carl said.

"I guess."

"Cool. See ya tomorrow." Carl hung up.

Maybe he shouldn't have told Carl about the grechtzoar.

Jimmy went into the bathroom. He squirted out a big pump of his mother's scented soap, pear with white tea. He inhaled the scent. It seemed like a girly thing to do, but it always calmed him. After washing his hands, Jimmy went into his bedroom and slid the dresser in front of his door. As he climbed into bed, he held his fragrant hands in front of his face and drifted off.

The next morning, Jimmy went outside to get his baseball glove. But though he searched under every bush, the glove had vanished.

"So you saw it around here?" Carl asked, adjusting his wristwatch. He'd set the alarm to beep an hour before sunset. When it played "Pop Goes the Weasel," it would be their signal to turn back. They stood at the forest's edge, holding their weapons. While Carl pushed his way between two bushes, Jimmy waited at the edge, his breathing shallow.

"Hey, look at this."

Jimmy hesitated. He held his hands near his face, catching a whiff of pear and white tea. The soap reminded him of his mother's bedroom: sunlit and safe, with a soft king-sized mattress where he used to crawl between his parents on Saturday mornings.

"Come on, check this out!"

Jimmy reluctantly pushed through the bushes, ducking the short branches. Carl shook his head. "Here, take this. You need it more." He handed Jimmy his favorite switchblade, the one his father had given him for his twelfth birthday.

"Thanks." Jimmy put the knife in his pocket, but it didn't make him feel any better. What good was a three-inch blade against a beast whose entire mouth was filled with teeth bigger than that?

"Droppings!" Carl said, poking a giant turd on the ground with a stick. "It's soft." It was large, the size of a Subway sandwich, and shaped eerily like a human's. Jimmy stared. The poking released a faint stench, like ham left in the refrigerator too long. A prickle of nausea rose through his stomach. Though it was a bright day, the sun felt cold. The pine trees rustled in the wind, their branches swaying as though shaking their heads in warning. Go back, they seemed to whisper. Go back.

But Carl would know he was a coward, and soon everyone at school would know, too. "Grechtzoar," they'd cough whenever he went by. The thought of enduring a cafeteria full of sneering eyes pushed Jimmy farther into the forest.

Jimmy spotted something on one of the trees further away and pointed. "Over there." One of the brittle lower branches dangled from its source, the snapped part a jagged edge. Caught on the splintered point was a black tuft of something. He picked it up.

The tuft felt like a scrap of cloth. It was frayed and packed with dirt. He handed it to Carl.

"It's fur," Carl declared. "It must be shedding."

They kept walking. Jimmy hoped they would be able to find their way back. It seemed like they had been walking in a straight line, but he couldn't tell for sure. The woods were bright and quiet, but Jimmy kept looking around, expecting to feel a row of sharp pink teeth sink into his ankle at any moment.

"Oh, shit." Carl gestured toward a tree up ahead. At the base of its trunk, flies buzzed around the mangled remains of a house cat. Its neck was broken, the stomach slashed, guts scattered some distance from the body as though the cat had been flung through the air.

Jimmy's legs felt weak. He turned away. Despite the light streaming down in thick, golden beams into the clearing, he didn't hear any insects or birds. Jimmy found it odd for the forest to be so silent. In the middle of the clearing sat a small wooden shed on raised legs. It had only three walls, and on the floor lay a battered seat that looked like it had come from a van. From nails on the interior walls hung ropes of various lengths.

"What the..." Jimmy whispered.

Carl took a step toward it, squinting. A cold feeling clamped its fingers around Jimmy's stomach. "Let's get out of here." He grabbed Carl's arm and tried to pull him back, but Carl shook him off.

"Wait, I want to see what it is."

Carl walked closer to the shed. Although his skin prickled, Jimmy wished he had his friend's bravery. Carl went right up to the platform and poked the chair with the pointed tip of his shears. He laughed as a cloud of dust rose.

"What do you think those ropes are for?" Carl asked.

A grunt and a crackling branch sounded behind Jimmy. While watching Carl, he'd forgotten to stay vigilant. Jimmy shifted his weight to run, but something heavy slammed into him and something else slammed into his head. His eyes opened to dirt and pine needles, their cold scent right in front of him. A dark shape rushed past, and he heard the sound of scuffling.

Jimmy tried to stand, but his legs lurched beneath him, and bright pinpricks of light showered before his eyes. Gritting his teeth, he tried to get up again and staggered to his feet. Carl screamed—short, high-pitched shrieks over and over. Jimmy's head throbbed. It surprised him to hear Carl making such a terrified sound. He'd lost the shovel, but he touched his pocket and felt the knife. Somehow, its calm weight told him he had to get out of there. Pushing through the dizzy weakness of his body, Jimmy ran.

His mother knelt in front of him, gripping his arms so tightly that it hurt. "Did you know him? What did he look like?"

"It wasn't a person. It was a—"

"A what?"

But Jimmy couldn't speak. He kept thinking of the dark shape, the thing that had rushed past him. The more he tried to remember, the more he was sure there'd been a tail, and a snout that probably remembered his scent.

The police investigator frowned and tried to ask the same questions he had before. "How tall was he? What color hair?"

"It was a grechtzoar," Jimmy said.

The investigator sat down and put on a patient face. "Listen, son, the first two days are the most important in a missing persons case. Anything you can remember will help us find your friend."

Jimmy clutched his arms across his stomach. "Carl is dead! I know it." He had the terrible feeling that it was true.

"Now, that's not necessarily the case. There's a good chance we could find him."

Jimmy shook his head. "Not alive, you won't."

It took them a week to locate the body. When the news story broke, kids at school started whispering. They looked at Jimmy like he was the grechtzoar—like he might start raving and biting any minute.

"He thinks a monster ate his friend. Now he's in therapy."

"How did he know Carl was dead? Maybe he's the one who did him in."

Jimmy's mom threw out the papers and hovered over him when he used the Internet at home. But he read everything online in the school library when he was supposed to be researching a science project.

First, the investigators discovered pieces in the woods: fingers, clumps of hair, an ear. They found the remains of the first boy covered in a tarp under leaves. Carl's torso lay nearby in a pile of leaves. His hands had been cut off, the shortened arms sprawled to each side, while the hands had been arranged on top of the body, the stumps placed together in a butterfly shape. The fingernails had been painted in a glittery white polish neatly, as though by a practiced expert.

Jimmy kept expecting to spot Carl in the halls at school, or to see his name pop up on his phone, even though he knew he was dead. Once, coming back from the bathroom, he saw a boy who looked just like his friend. He had the same shaggy brown hair as Carl, the same cargo pants, the same lanky stride. Suddenly, Jimmy wondered if everyone had been wrong. After all, it had been a closed casket funeral. Maybe it was all a conspiracy, and Carl was still alive. A tendril of hope curled up through his stomach.

Jimmy followed him. The boy turned a corner, and Jimmy scurried to catch up. "Carl?" he called. "Carl, wait up!"

The boy walked faster. Jimmy started jogging. Then the boy ran, too. Jimmy chased him. Finally, outside a classroom, he caught up.

"Hey, Carl! Why are you running away?" He cornered the boy and grabbed him, wrenching him around.

"Leave me alone!" the boy screamed. "Please!" His voice came out loud and shrill. The sound of screaming made Jimmy's blood race, and he jumped back. He had heard a scream like that before; he was in danger.

His hand flew to his right pocket, where the weight of Carl's knife promised safety. In an instant, it filled his hand, the blade unfurled and pointed in the direction of the threat. The screaming grew louder. Someone grabbed his arms with cold hands and dragged him back. Someone else pinned him on the floor. Kids stared at him from the classroom door, and a teacher scribbled something on a pad of paper. Someone dragged him to the principal's office. Then his mother drove him home frowning, asking what on earth she was supposed to do.

The suspension infuriated his mother, but Jimmy refused to apologize. He had needed Carl's knife. Even when he was in the corner of the classroom where no one could sneak up on him, he always felt short of breath and tense. Having his hand on the cool, smooth metal was the only thing that made him feel better.

On the first day, after his mother left for work, he crept downstairs and dragged the tall stool next to the refrigerator. He groped around for the cardboard box where she always kept confiscated items. His fingers touched plastic things, clumps of dust, and something round and sticky he flicked away in disgust. Finally, in the back, he felt it: a rectangle of metal, weighty to the touch. As he grasped it, its steady coolness spread through him. He had a lot to do.

The need to make people believe him drove Jimmy. The grechtzoar was on the loose, ready to eat another kid any day now. Jimmy thought about the attack in the forest. He should've kept a better lookout, should've gotten up faster, shouldn't have run away. Now all he could do was prove that Carl hadn't been killed by some ordinary guy. The grechtzoar was much worse than any man. Every night, Jimmy dreamed about matted fur, eyes flashing in the darkness, black noses sniffing the ground for boys.

The police liked crime sketches, so maybe a picture would convince them. The handbook didn't have any; he'd have to draw it himself. He ran upstairs to his room and took out a fresh 8.5x11 sheet of paper. After an hour, he managed to produce close-ups of certain parts—a tail, a tooth, a claw—but not the beast in its entirety.

Facts from the handbook drifted into his mind:

It hunts for pleasure, not need—for the joy of tearing flesh, and feeling the life twitch slowly out of a warm body.

It can live for up to eighty years.

Just before death, its eyes darken and it lays a black egg. By the time the baby hatches, the corpse is stiff and dull-eyed, a perfect source of food.

Ignoring the rest, Jimmy attempted the eyes, then erased one and brushed the pink shreds off the paper. He made them bigger. They still didn't look right. He crumpled the drawing up and threw it away.

Jimmy reached for his handbook, hidden under some papers on his desk. The only solution was to find Herb Flaherty, the only person who would know what to do. He tried the number in the handbook one last time, but only reached the same canned message as usual. The number was disconnected. Disappointment settled like a lump of snow in his stomach.

Jimmy sighed and flipped the pages from one side of the book to the other. The paperback spine had cracked open to the spot with the grechtzoar, the pages stained with candy they'd eaten from the secret stash under Carl's bed. They used to sit in his room and study their handbooks together, saying which creatures were lame and which ones were awesome. Flipping to the back, Jimmy thought he saw something in the pages. He turned them slowly, looking for what he'd seen. A piece of paper folded in half slipped from between the last few pages and fell into Jimmy's lap.

The font and color looked familiar. He opened it. In the upper left-hand corner was an inscription in sloppy handwriting he had seen before. Carl Jenkins. A chill ran across his skin. The missing page from Carl's book, the one with Herb Flaherty's contact information. Carl had drawn a squiggly line under the phone number and highlighted it in blue. Jimmy read it twice. Something was different. He checked his phone for calls dialed. 555-920-4567. He checked the number in the book. 4568.

Jimmy flipped the page over, discovering the title—Herb Flaherty's Handbook: Revised and Expanded Edition.

Everything people had said about Carl's death went through his mind—how they thought Jimmy was crazy, how he made everything up. But the grechtzoar was on the loose, probably stalking its next prey right at this instant. People needed to know the truth.

He knew the first part of the phone number by memory but double-checked to make sure he typed 8 at the end before hitting send. He held his breath until the phone rang.

"Hello?" The voice on the other end was deep and hoarse. Jimmy almost dropped the phone, surprised anyone had answered.

"Hello? Anyone there?"

"Yeah, I just, I—"

"Who is this?"

Jimmy thought of what Carl would do. "I'm calling to report a grechtzoar sighting. It was on October fourth. It was—a boy was killed."

There was a pause at the other end. "You were there when it happened?"

"Yes."

The man didn't say anything, so Jimmy kept talking. "I'm worried it might come back, but no one believes me. They say there's no evidence."

He heard a rush of air that sounded like a snort. "No evidence? The grechtzoar must have done a good job covering up its crime."

"Can monsters do that?"

Something crackled over the phone. The man whispered, "Some monsters can. And believe me, the grechtzoar is a very special monster."

"I need to stop it. Can you help me?"

"Can I help you," the man mused, as though considering whether he could truly help. He chuckled. "Or maybe the question is, can you help me?" His voice changed, became brisk and abrupt. "Have you ever seen a grechtzoar skull, Jimmy? Or its teeth?"

"No." Jimmy didn't remember telling the man his name, but maybe he was mistaken.

"Why don't you come visit me this afternoon? Then we can talk."

The address the man—Flaherty— gave was just a half mile from Jimmy's house. When he saw it on the map, a knot of guilt lodged in his throat. If only he and Carl had called Herb before tracking the grechtzoar. But it was too late for that now.

After school, Jimmy followed the map to a narrow dirt road that jutted into the forest. He could barely breathe, and his neck felt as tense as a coiled spring. With each birdcall and crackling twig, he tightened his grip on the switchblade in his pocket until it hurt.

The house hunched, isolated in a grove of trees. Uneven shingled siding covered its sides like thinning feathers, and crooked black shutters hung at odd angles from the windows. Jimmy squinted at the tarnished numbers by the door, confirming the address. He tried to feel brave, like Carl, but his hands shook as he trudged through the weeds and up the crumbling, moss-covered stoop.

Jimmy stood there for a second, fighting the urge to run. He held his palm to his face and took a deep breath. The soapy scent was sweet and soothing. So what if the house looked a little strange? He was here to learn the truth about the grechtzoar. Carl wouldn't want him to be a chicken. He raised his hand to the knocker and struck three sharp raps.

The door creaked open. Behind it, Jimmy saw the glare of glasses, a mustache, a balding head. The man stood there for a second, not opening the door further or coming out to greet him.

"You must be Jimmy."

"How do you know my name?"

Herb smiled. "It doesn't happen very often, that kids come to visit me."

Jimmy fidgeted and looked back to the deserted road. He wondered if this entire plan was somehow a mistake.

"Hang on, don't move," Herb said. "I'm enjoying this moment." It felt like he was staring at him, but Jimmy couldn't quite tell because Herb's glasses were so thick. Jimmy thought about running away, but worried it might be rude.

"Okay, okay. Where are my manners? Come in. Have a seat." Herb stepped back and let Jimmy in, gesturing to the living room.

It took a moment for Jimmy's eyes to adjust—all of the shades were drawn. Puffy yellow chairs sat around a coffee table. In each corner stood display cabinets full of shells, feathers, and small animal skulls. Jimmy chose a chair by the far wall.

He heard the sound of a bolt clicking into place. Jimmy whipped around to see Herb depositing a key in his pocket. When he saw Jimmy watching, he chuckled.

"Had a break-in a few weeks ago. Don't want that to happen again."

There had been a string of break-ins around town, but even so, Jimmy felt uneasy. Herb came over and sat in the chair across from him. "I'm so glad you came to ask about the grechtzoar. Out of all the creatures I write about, it's my favorite."

"It attacked my friend," Jimmy said. "It—it killed him." It was hard to say, but Carl would've been proud. He felt like his friend was nearby but hiding, maybe behind the chair or next to the bookcase.

"That's too bad." The way Herb said it, they could've been talking about the weather. Jimmy had expected Herb to be more upset about the death, but that wasn't what mattered. Carl would've wanted him to complete the mission.

Jimmy leaned forward. "I need to know if there's any way to stop the grechtzoar. I think it might attack someone else."

"Stop the grechtzoar," Herb said, leaning back thoughtfully in his chair. "Yes, it will most certainly attack again." He chuckled. "What a fascinating beast. For instance, did you know the first grechtzoar came from a human mother? She expected to have a baby, but instead, out came this strange, black egg." He smiled as though the egg were his own personal achievement.

"Huh," Jimmy said, somewhere between anxious and angry. Herb didn't fit the figure he and Carl had imagined wrote the guide. "The handbook says it remembers your scent. Is there any way to make it forget?"

"Make it forget?" Herb said, smiling and sniffing the air. "Not likely. You know what it really likes? Soaps. It finds those very attractive. Once it gets a scent, it never forgets. No other animal would become so...obsessed."

"Don't you have any evidence?" Jimmy asked. He had come all this way, and now Herb ran him in circles. "I thought you mentioned a skull or something."

"Indeed, I have a skull." Herb went to a cabinet in the corner and opened it.

Jimmy studied the bookcase next to his chair. Bottles of nail polish filled the upper shelf in a rainbow of colors. Now that he looked more closely, the lower shelf didn't have skulls like the others, but instead contained random objects: a soccer trophy, a doll, a hair brush. A baseball glove.

Herb came back with a small skull in one hand and a plastic shopping bag in the other. He placed the bag by his feet and held the skull out to Jimmy. "Take a look."

It was the size of a cat's, small enough to fit in one hand. It didn't even have sharp teeth, only short flat ones. If this was the only evidence of the grechtzoar, no one would ever believe him.

Jimmy turned it over skeptically. "Is this really a grechtzoar? It seems so tiny."

"It's a baby one." Herb sounded amused, but Jimmy couldn't really tell because the room was so dark. He looked at the windows, wondering if he could climb out of one if he had to.

"What's wrong?" Herb asked, sounding hurt. Jimmy wondered if he had judged too harshly. He wasn't sure what, exactly, made him so nervous. Guilt welled up in his chest, and he put the grechtzoar skull back down on the coffee table.

"Is there anything else in that bag?" Maybe it held teeth or claws, anything else that might prove the grechtzoar was real.

Herb smiled. "I'm glad you asked." He opened the bag and laid the contents on the coffee table. There was another plastic shopping bag and a few pieces of rope.

"I don't get it. Is this for trapping the grechtzoar?"

"You'll see."

Somewhere, a wristwatch beeped. The sound came from the shelf with the nail polish playing a tune that Jimmy recognized: "Pop Goes the Weasel." He sat up straighter. The cheerful melody hit his ears like ice. Carl's watch.

"Maybe I should get going," Jimmy said. He jumped out of his chair. Herb's head swiveled toward him. Because the glasses were so cloudy, he couldn't tell the exact focus of Herb's eyes. Jimmy took a step around the coffee table, but Herb blocked his path.

"What's the rush? Don't you want to learn more about the grechtzoar?"

Jimmy wondered how long it would take him to slip the knife out of his pocket. "I need to go. My mom's expecting me." If he kicked Herb in the groin, it might give him a chance to escape. He brought his knee up, but Herb knocked it aside, coming close, forcing Jimmy back into the chair.

"You have such nice hands." He reached for one of Jimmy's wrists, but Jimmy jerked it away. "They smell so good. You like scents, don't you, Jimmy? Kind of like the grechtzoar."

"I need to leave," Jimmy said, his throat as tight as that moment when the grechtzoar came up behind him in the woods. It felt like drowning in the air.

"Not so fast," Herb said. "Don't you know why I wrote the handbook?"

Jimmy stared at him.

"So I could meet kids just like you." Herb grabbed one of the plastic bags and pieces of rope and moved toward him.

"Stop."

Herb seized Jimmy's wrist.

"No!" Jimmy tried to wrench his arm away, but Herb yanked him closer and whispered.

"Carl fought harder than that."

Jimmy felt like he'd been swimming in shallow water, only to put his feet down and realize he'd slipped over the edge of a terrible black abyss. The grechtzoar wasn't real. It never had been. In its place was the truth, this man, much worse than any monster. As Jimmy realized he would never feel safe again, hot rage swept through him. With his free hand, he grabbed the switchblade, popped it open, and plunged it into Herb's ribcage.

"Take that!"

Herb screamed and let go, pressing his hand to his side. A red puddle bloomed across his shirt. Jimmy swatted the glasses off his face and stabbed him again. Herb sank to his knees, his eyes pale and bulging, milky white, with no visible irises.

Jimmy darted around Herb and snatched the watch from the cabinet shelf. The front door was locked, so he ran down the hallway into the kitchen, where a screen door led to the porch outside. He heard Herb stumbling after him. Jimmy tried the door and discovered it locked. He fumbled with the latch. Something snapped, but the door stayed stuck. He kicked it desperately, and it clattered open.

Jimmy ran and ran, his lungs burning; his legs felt like they would fall off. He was almost to his house. Soon he saw it, the yellow one with red shutters. He grabbed the key from under the mat and unlocked the door and dashed inside, just like he'd practiced so many times before.

As he slammed the door and bolted it, he turned around to see his mother staring at him. "Oh God! What happened?" She rushed over to Jimmy, her hands pressed to the sides of her face.

Wordlessly, Jimmy handed her Carl's watch.

COUNTERPOINT

When John woke up on Friday morning, he found himself on the couch next to his piano, still wearing yesterday's clothes. He lifted his head, and his stiff neck screamed at him. Looking down at his hands, he discovered ink stained his fingers. Crumpled sheets of staff paper lay scattered across the floor. Bach's disapproving face hung in a gilded frame on the wall.

Sylvia had not stayed with him last night. The week before, she'd come to pack the clothes she kept on her side of the closet. Her Gardiner CDs and high heels were gone, even her spare nail clippers. She hated having her nails too long. They interfered when she played the violin.

The engagement ring he had never given her still sat in its box behind the piano's music stand, a thin band with a small diamond, the best he could afford on his meager church organist's salary. John stood and pressed his forehead to the window. Outside, a meadow of milkweed and Queen Anne's lace swayed in the light breeze. Beyond the narrow road, a red barn floated over a cornfield like a ship far out at sea. Swallows dipped through the air, catching insects. Here, unlike in the city, the sky was unobstructed and endless.

Two months ago, things had still been perfect. After Sylvia returned from her Paris audition, John drove her to Lake Winnebago to distract her from the anxiety of waiting. Usually, he listened to Die Kunst der Fuge in the car, but for her, he put on Tchaikovsky's Fifth Symphony. By the second movement, Sylvia sang; during the triumphant fourth, she pretended to conduct. John turned the volume up and rolled the windows down. He glanced at her in the passenger seat, her black hair whipping against her pale skin.

It rained earlier that day, but by the time they reached the lighthouse, the storm had subsided, leaving damp earth and luminous puddles. Holding Sylvia's hand, John looked into a reflection: the two of them, the lighthouse, plump clouds in hues of rose and amethyst. He saw Sylvia's smile. A breeze rippled the surface, and the image vanished.

<hr />

John gathered the scattered manuscript sheets and went to his car. Outside, he heard minor triads in the hum of insects' wings, a soundtrack for regret. He drove down the slim ribbon of road to church. The church's white siding glowed in the sunlight, with a tall steeple that housed a clock tower. He parked in the back lot next to the cemetery, where his grandparents and great-grandparents slept under faded stones.

Inside, the stained-glass windows cast rose and lavender patches across the carpeted floor. John walked across the altar and switched on the organ. It emitted a moan as wind crept into the bellows. Standing behind the bench, he pressed one note, then another: C, D, E. He admired how each step and half-step led to the next, how the scale itself was a perfect musical creation.

Sliding onto the bench, he spread his fingers across the pale golden keys. Perched next to the console was the old-fashioned metronome Sylvia had given him two years ago. It had to be wound with a key. No matter how many times John turned the key, it would inevitably slow and stop.

He smoothed the sheets of staff paper and tried to discern what he'd written. He started the piece yesterday: a fugue, a work of counterpoint with up to four simultaneous lines of music. The theme had come from Sylvia's voice, the melody in the way she said, "I'm moving."

John tested new measures, adjusted them, transcribed. Composition only half-distracted him from the agitated thought of what he would do tomorrow when he saw Sylvia at the wedding. There had to be something he could do to change her mind.

***

John was shocked when Sylvia won the Paris audition. She called him as soon as she found out, her voice high-pitched with joy. She had always wanted to play with a major symphony, but after years of failed auditions, John stopped paying attention to her attempts. He quietly bought the ring, waiting only for the right moment to ask.

It was not that he doubted her talent. Her Bach violin partitas were the best he had heard. He listened to her play them in the sanctuary, early on one of the Sundays they were to perform together. His arms chilled when he heard Bach's perfect counterpoint, as though the composer were alive and watching. Sylvia rocked back and forth as she played, biting the corner of her lip. Her fingers flitted like shafts of light across the neck of the violin.

Sylvia failed professional auditions for years, sabotaged by crippling anxiety. When nerves seized her, she couldn't remember the opening measures of the Mendelssohn concerto. Her fingers sweated and slid; she made Mozart sound like Schoenberg.

John met her at a gig performing Fauré's Requiem. During a rehearsal break, he watched Sylvia practice, and the clarity of her playing struck him. He introduced himself, and they kept talking long after the rehearsal. Her boldness, her refusal to give up on music, attracted him. She liked that he composed, that his ambition was to write pieces worthy of his idol, Bach. They saw each other on weekends, either at his home in the small town where he'd always lived or at her apartment in Madison. Occasionally, John would realize an entire year had passed. Time fell away in large chunks, like accumulated snow plunging suddenly from a rooftop.

While John settled into quiet routine, Sylvia auditioned for big symphonies. She flew to Philadelphia, Atlanta, Los Angeles. When those failed, she traveled to Sydney and Berlin. Secretly, John hoped after a critical mass of failures she would stop trying to escape.

The day before she flew to her Paris audition, he drove the hour to her apartment in Madison, a spare one-bedroom decorated with a single orchid plant in the window. Her rolling suitcase was already packed. He cooked dinner, sat with her on the couch, and stroked her hair, saying it would be all right. She didn't seem as nervous as usual.

Later, he went into the bathroom and saw her lavender toiletry bag open on the bathroom counter. On top, conspicuous among tubes of makeup, lay a stout orange bottle of pills: beta blockers.

For some reason, the revelation upset John, though many musicians used them. He picked up the bottle. The pills didn't rattle; the bottle was stuffed with cotton. He could slip it into his pocket, but he thought about Sylvia checking into her hotel. She would take out her violin. She'd rub the bow with rosin and play a few notes. Her hands would shake. She'd look for the bottle and realize it wasn't there.

John put the bottle back. How much could a pill really do? There was no way she would win.

John had been composing for hours before someone interrupted him. On Friday afternoons, a church lady always came to vacuum the rugs. She chirped a greeting.

"You ready for the wedding?" she asked.

He nodded. The life of an organist was filled with providing background for other people's weddings. This time it was the pastor's daughter, marrying a deacon's son. The whole church was invited. The daughter requested that Sylvia play a particular favorite, Lieder ohne Worte. While the woman vacuumed, John rested, let his eyes unfocus and wander across the blurred notes on the page. If he finished this piece, this piece that he had based on Sylvia's voice, he could somehow convince her to stay and listen. If she stayed, he would have a chance to show her the ring. He would show it and she would realize, at least for a moment, what she meant to him.

After Sylvia won the audition, she came bursting through his door. "I can't believe it! It's incredible!" Her green eyes were wide, catching the light.

"I'm so proud of you," he said, trying to inject enthusiasm into his voice. He went to the kitchen to fetch her a glass of her favorite raspberry lemonade. He found it too sweet for his liking, but he always kept it in the fridge for her. In their four years together, he had never seen her this excited. From the living room, he heard Sylvia at the piano. She picked out the opening of Bach's fugue in C-sharp major from The Well-Tempered Clavier. With seven sharps in the key signature, it had an especially bright timbre. The cheerful sound grated on John's nerves.

He went in and set her glass on the coffee table. Sylvia had pushed aside a stack of staff paper to sit on the piano bench. To her, the arrangement may have looked random, but it was the sheets of a composition John had been working on.

"I've always wanted to live in Paris," Sylvia said. "You could get a job in a real cathedral, with stained glass."

John stiffened. "My church has stained glass."

"But wouldn't it be—"

"What makes you think I want to move?"

Sylvia turned to look at him. "It's Paris."

"I hate cities."

But it was more than that. John had lived the entirety of his thirty-six years in Wisconsin. How could she think so little of his life, to assume he'd be happy to throw it away for France?

"John," Sylvia said, anxious now. She came over to him. "I didn't mean to assume. I thought you'd be excited, too." She wrapped her arms around him. "We'll visit for a few days, see if you like it. If not, you'll come right back here, okay?"

John nodded, unwillingly at first, but when Sylvia made a silly face and tickled him, he couldn't help laughing. Maybe a visit wouldn't be so bad. Maybe he would even like it. Half an hour later, he sat at the piano. Sylvia took out her violin, tuned it, and improvised a melody over the chords John played. When John nodded for a cadence, Sylvia ended with a flourish, like she had just finished playing a concerto.

She set her violin in the open case. John took her hands and led her to the tattered couch. Sylvia shrugged off her sweater and laughed softly as John ran his hands through her hair, fresh with the scent of shampoo. Her lashes were long and black, her skin almost translucent, like white jade. John kissed her at the opening of her blouse. He traced the base of her neck with his thumb. He kissed her on the nose, at the ear, on the small dark mole near the base of her collarbone.

When the light faded from the sanctuary, John drove home. He entered his dim house and saw what a mess it had become. Sheets of crumpled paper lay by the piano, flanked by cast-off shoes and food-stained dishes. Still, over the last few hours, he convinced himself that once Sylvia heard his music and saw the ring, things could work out.

He spread out the staff paper on the piano's music stand. The dour portrait of Bach, clutching a rolled-up sheet of music, stared at him from the wall above. John's fugue neared completion. From the original melody in Sylvia's voice, it evolved into a thirty-minute sprawl of fantasy and counterpoint. The notes sprawled across the page, hundreds of little black dots all over the paper, arranged on five-line staves in melodies, harmonies, and moments of exquisite polyphony. As John continued the fugue, he imagined himself inside its two-dimensional architectures, in the world contained by the notes as if it were a physical reality: a labyrinth, a palace, a castle.

He played and felt his body withdraw from the outer world, retreating into his inner musical fantasy: major and minor shifting like sun and shadow through the windows of his mad king's castle, as outside, the wind rushed clouds above the earth—or perhaps it was the earth rushing ahead, spinning wildly through space, clouds streaming like cast-off flags behind.

The Paris trip had been a disaster. In retrospect, John didn't know why he had been hopeful when even Madison proved too much for him, the city noises like knives in his ears. On the plane flight, he gripped Sylvia's hand so hard, she told him to let go; it was her playing hand. At the hotel, he froze at hearing a language he could not understand. While Sylvia flitted from the Sacré-Coeur to Notre Dame, dragging him along, John imagined the meadow outside his house to stop himself from panicking in the noisy crowds of tourists. He felt the irrational fear that he would somehow die in France, an ocean away from his home. "I can't do this," John said on the last evening in the hotel.

"So it's you or Paris?" Sylvia said.

He didn't like the harshness of that statement, but it was true. He nodded.

"I thought you supported me. I've been working for this my whole life."

"I do support you. But I can't live here." Then he said something he regretted. "I didn't think you would use beta blockers." It had bothered him ever since he'd seen the bottle. Three hundred years ago, in the honest age of Bach—even a few decades ago—there had been no anxiety drugs. A musician could play under pressure or not.

"What's that supposed to mean?" She slapped a palm on the dresser. "I'm not allowed to advance my career? You want me to stay prisoner in your backwater state? How did you even know I used them?"

"I saw them in your bag," John said, realizing how suspicious this sounded. "It was on the counter."

Sylvia snorted. "Maybe this move is for the best."

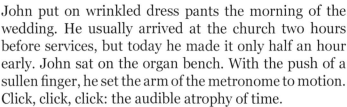

John put on wrinkled dress pants the morning of the wedding. He usually arrived at the church two hours before services, but today he made it only half an hour early. John sat on the organ bench. With the push of a sullen finger, he set the arm of the metronome to motion. Click, click, click: the audible atrophy of time.

He looked in the mirror above his music stand, watching for Sylvia. He hoped she would look distraught, showing physical signs of distress. Fifteen minutes later, she glided through the doors at the back, defiantly beautiful in a sleek blazer and chiffon blouse, wearing her favorite high heels that revealed a few inches of her feet. She sat down in a chair near the piano at the front and took out her violin. She tuned the strings, carefully adjusting each fifth. He played a few hymns to warm up, staring into the mirror to see if she ever glanced in his direction. She did not.

For the processional, John played mechanically while the bridesmaids marched down the aisle, one after another like grotesque parade floats. There was the bride, white and ethereal. At the edge of his vision, Sylvia swept the bow over the strings, rocking back and forth as always. John felt like he was burning during all the talk about love. What did they mean when they said love was kind, and all other saintly things? His love was selfish—wanting to keep her a geographical prisoner—but that did not diminish its reality.

After the recessional, everyone filed out. Sylvia, free of company, wiped the neck of her violin with a cloth. John went down to talk to her. Strapping the violin into its case, she didn't notice him standing behind her.

"Sylvia," he said. She turned to look at him. Though he had imagined what he would say hundreds of times, he couldn't remember a single word.

"John?"

"I wrote a piece," he said. "Want to hear it?"

She checked her watch. "I have a few minutes."

As he played, his hands sweated and shook over the keys. He missed notes and hit clashing harmonies he hadn't written. But he was confident she would hear the soul of it, the longing and regret. When he finished, he would tell her it had all come from her voice.

He was on the second to last page when he felt her hand on his shoulder. He took his hands off the keys. The major chord he had just played rang in the sanctuary and faded.

"John, I have to go. My flight's at three."

"Your flight?"

"To Paris." She looked at him with pity, as though he were too stupid to remember what had happened. "Bye, I guess."

"Wait." She watched as he took the small box out of his pocket. She shook her head before he even opened it. "It's not going to work," she said. "Good-bye, John." She turned and walked out of the sanctuary.

Good-bye, John. Three words ended, so swiftly, four years. In the parking lot, he sat in his car, watching others leave until only he remained. There had been a melody in those words, as there always was in Sylvia's voice. He took a crumpled napkin and a pen from the glove compartment. He scribbled five lines for a musical staff and transcribed the melody.

At home, he opened the piano bench. He thrust aside his Bärenreiter edition of The Well-Tempered Clavier. He hardly ever used it anyway; all the preludes and fugues lived in the memory of his fingers.

He smoothed the napkin and took out a fresh sheet of paper. Five-lined staves stretched horizontally across. The sheet was blank with possibilities, but the portrait of Bach stared down at him, disapproving. He copied the melody onto the paper with a mechanical pencil, then sat and stared. He played the first measure a few times on the piano. He listened and listened but couldn't hear the notes that came next.

HIDING GAME

She looks for his face in the faces of others: for tanned skin and dark almond eyes; for stark eyebrows over long, soft lashes. She watches for briskness of step, toned biceps, short legs. In crowds she spots pieces of him—back of head, sharp profile, crossed arms—but always the subject moves in a foreign way, revealing himself a stranger.

Six months have passed since he failed to arrive at her place. He neglected calls, texts, and emails. She flooded his phone with voicemails until the inbox was full. He had recently given her the key to his apartment, so she traveled forty minutes by bus and took the elevator to the fifth floor. She jiggled the key in the lock and swung the door wide open, calling his name.

The leather couch stood in its place by the window, flanked by the glass coffee table. In the bedroom, the powder blue comforter stretched neatly across the mattress. She opened a dresser drawer: all socks matched, all boxers folded. She checked under the bed, in the closets, behind doors. He was nowhere. The only clue: a tentative layer of dust on all surfaces, smooth and undisturbed.

Now, six months later, the police have no leads. Maybe they're in on it, this hiding game, this elaborate joke that might end with a reveal, laughter, relief. Maybe she'll discover it was all a mistake, an erroneous address, digits of the apartment transposed—and he, down the hall, waiting.

She feels his presence nearby, warm and watching. She hears his voice when she drives alone, his admiration when she sheds clothes for a shower. When she presses her nose into his gray cashmere sweater, she can catch his scent. He's here, somewhere not far from this place. Eventually, she is sure, she will find him.

DO IT WITH
SOMEONE YOU LOVE

We stride through the quad in a phalanx, our hands in the pockets of our pastel pants, our jackets flapping in the September afternoon air. Derrick has called a meeting. We have to be at the house by four.

In the corner of the green lawn, just across the street from frat row, they're having an outdoor self-defense seminar. A short-haired woman with the female symbol tattooed on her bicep glares at us. She yells into the microphone to say no first, then kick us in the balls if necessary. It's laughable. Only about five girls sit around her. And let's face it, they look like the type who'll spend this Friday sequestered in their own bedrooms, watching chaste foreign films where boys and girls hold hands. Even if they came to our house, we'd turn them away. They're too chubby, too pale, too earnest. No one wants to party with girls like that.

"Hey, ladies," we call as we pass by, just to see them whip their heads around, stare at us as though we're villains.

The girls we like thrive elsewhere. They're little lithe things stuttering down the sidewalks in heels. Their dresses, covering just a few inches of their thighs, flip up in the wind. They giggle and smooth their skirts with uncertain hands. Their fingernails are cherry blossom pink, and their eyes are ringed with makeup, wet and dark like bruises.

We're the freshman pledge class. We roam the campus in a pack, never alone, always proud. Soon, we'll make this place ours. But first, we must prove our devotion, surmount one final task to become official brothers.

The living room is the grandest in the house with wood paneling, a crimson carpet, a chandelier, and old portraits on the walls. Last year, my big brother tells me, a drunken, jilted junior plunged his fist into the smug face of Josiah Eldridge IV—hence the glass cases now protecting the survivors. Derrick hasn't arrived yet. We joke about the manly female college president, whose name, Jordan, is appropriately ambiguous.

A silence settles into the spaces of our conversation. Our older comrades smile in anticipation. We, the pledges, try to match their ease, but a twitching eyebrow on one face, a strained grin on another, betray our wariness. We know we're not brothers yet. We know we still might fail.

"Pledges," Derrick says, striding through the door and holding out his hands like he's a candidate up for election. He likes showy entrances, and his voice always sounds like it's booming from a podium. "Tonight. Your first official party. The party where we'll see how you represent us. Where we'll see if you can act like real men."

We stir in the places where we stand, aware we're still separate, still not men. In the name of acting like real men, we downed two cases of beer and several handles of vodka last weekend. Our stomachs shivered when we looked into the bitter depths of our sixth and seventh glasses, but discomfort and nausea were a small price for the title of men. If all ten of us drank, then we could reach the pledges' quota. All ten of us shared the burden, as we hoped soon to share this house, share everything.

"This picture," Derrick says, holding up his phone, "was taken last weekend." He raises his eyebrows. "After hours." A few of the older brothers laugh even before he passes them the phone. They study the picture with familiar connoisseurship, pointing out details previously unnoticed, savoring the composition.

The picture shouldn't surprise us, but it does. A blond in a short, hot pink dress is face down on a twin bed, her feet on the floor. Her hair hides her face. The skirt of her dress is flipped up. Against her spread legs are a man's bare thighs and trim waist, anonymous except for the tattoo of a rose just above his hip bone. We wonder if this is the reason Derrick got the tattoo—so he would be identifiable even in photographs such as these. We wonder who took the picture.

"My friends, there are two things a man must know how to do. The first is drink. The other—" He pauses and grins. "Is girls."

———

Pics or it didn't happen. These words spread in whispers among us as we button our shirts, gel our hair, slip our feet into well-worn loafers. We all know what Derrick really means: do this, or leave. His directive excludes the possibility of invention, exaggeration, or anonymous transgression. None of us has a well-placed tattoo.

The ten of us feign bravado, make bets on who'll be first to succeed and who'll be last. Westin will probably win. He's always been the shoo-in, a former Senator's son. He looks like he spent his whole life on the beach with rumpled blond hair and blue eyes winking from his tanned face. Drew is the opposite. When we first saw him among the punches, we thought he'd be a threat. He's the massive star quarterback of the football team with hands as big as sauce pans. But he's actually a softie, and therefore weak. He can't pass homeless people in the square without giving them money, and he volunteers to take class notes for the deaf. As we talk about how to get girls, his smile slips off his face like oil off the surface of water. His hands are already shaking.

We can't bring ourselves to eat much dinner, though we know we should since we'll be drinking later. Through the windows of the dining hall, we watch the fading pink light. The quad looks like a storybook scene with blurry watercolor images of trees, green grass, and gray, gothic buildings with rosette windows. Those of us from cities remember how the glass skyscrapers look fiery orange in those last rays, pink and purple clouds visible in the gaps between buildings. Those of us from mountains think of how the sunset makes the bark of pine trees glow red. Our mothers are probably cooking chicken and mashed potatoes this instant. Images of home form a sharp twist in our hearts, a longing we shove away before it makes us less strong.

Our fathers took us out just before we left for school. We accepted offers from their alma mater, bought furniture, parted with friends, packed the car. We went to our dads' favorite dim-lit bars with orange-glowing windows where they ordered vodka tonics and a soda for us, the sons. They tipped some of the alcohol into our glasses before holding up a toast.

"I'm proud of you," they said. "You worked hard. You earned this. But there's something you need to know."

They tell us the truth about life. Things in the real world aren't like high school, where the kid with the highest GPA gets valedictorian, and the fastest and strongest get varsity. In real life, there are more talented people than there are spots for them. It isn't just about who's the best. The people who get things—the right jobs; therefore the right amount of money, the right house, right wife, and so on—are the people who have the right networks.

Networks, that mysterious adult word. It reminds us of AP biology, where we learned the largest organism on earth isn't a blue whale or an elephant, but a mushroom. The mushroom patch may appear to be made up of individuals, but it's actually a network with roots connecting each sprout underground. A single mushroom can weigh up to thousands of pounds.

Networks, our fathers tell us, are how they got their first job at the bank. They're how we know the lawyers who find our tax loopholes, and the doctors who take special care of our mothers when they get biopsies after false-positive mammograms.

And how do our fathers know all these people?

It all starts in college, they say. It all starts with joining the right crowd.

This assignment, we tell ourselves, is just a moment. It's just a moment in time, and then it's over.

Once it's dark, we stir. Friday night: when college students break their chrysalises of concentration and shed concerns about grades, majors, careers. It's a collective surrender to forgetfulness, a mass instinct to revel. There's buoyancy even in the steps of bespectacled unfortunates who've never had a drink. There's also true magic in the ones who flock the sidewalks of frat row, guys with dapper good looks and just a touch of cologne; girls in short, tight dresses, brightly colored like a bouquet of flowers.

Girls trip down bus steps and up the path to our house. Their voices sound eager notes in the darkness. They wear fabrics that catch the light: leather mini-dresses, sequin-covered tops, metallic skirts flashing blue and red. They swarm toward us in packs. For a moment, we hope there's enough alcohol, but then we remember how Derrick always thinks of everything.

Two girls hobble up our path in stilettos with six-inch heels. Westin greets them at the door, and three more of us crowd around them. There's something special about these two: perhaps their vulnerability, their obvious youth and dependence on each other, clinging to each other's elbows. Perhaps it's how they laugh and won't really look at us, darting their eyes to the side as we welcome them. The brunette wears white, and the blond wears black, perfect complements, as though their friendship were arranged for just this aesthetic purpose.

We each get a girl a red plastic cup of "punch." It's stronger than beer, liquor mixed with lots of fruit juice so they can't taste how much they're drinking. We've tried to convince ourselves that we like the smell of alcohol, pungent and primal, now permeating the entire house. The music thumps so loud we have to lean in and shout to ask the girls their names. We think they say Kate and Kat, but we're not exactly sure.

"Chatting up the ladies," Derrick shouts into our ears. "Good work—so far." Then he disappears like a wraith. We remember what he told us earlier. Freshmen are easy, drunk girls are easier. Drunk is practically a prerequisite. They're much less likely to say no.

"What if they do say no?" Drew asks. The rest of us roll our eyes. Leave it to Drew to ask the one stupid question.

"Evaluate the situation. Sometimes, if a girl says no? She doesn't really mean it." Derrick grins, as though he had experienced such a situation himself.

We dance. That's what this music is best for. We feel it in our chests like it's beating inside our ribs. We dance in the dark next to the girls with their breath hot on our shoulders, their faces so close we could kiss them. But before we try, they turn around, pressing their backs into us. We hold our hands out to the sides, pumping to the beat. Our hips meet theirs, accidentally at first, then intentionally. They seem to like it; they push back and rub. Their hair is in our faces, and our hands are on their hips. This is the fun part. Nothing's happened yet. Everything might happen, but we still don't know for sure.

We refill them on seconds, thirds, fourths, and some of us pull girls away into the dark.

We all know that one older guy, never our fathers, who's totally in love with his wife. Some of these women are hot, still wearing tight minis and lining their eyes with dark makeup. Most aren't. They're soccer moms in jeans and T-shirts with sweaty faces, just starting to show wrinkles on their foreheads. We don't get it. These men are blissed out, like they've found the perfect drug with no side effects. "Still as beautiful the day I met her," they say. "Look at her smile."

We're skeptical. These men tend to be teachers and nurses. They live in houses with peeling paint, and their cars look like they're about to fall apart on the road.

If we don't impress Derrick, if we're rejected from the fraternity, we'll be all alone in college, and in life. We'll have to befriend the leftovers, the poor and unconnected. And where will that get us? We know how many college grads these days can't find work, or slave away for minimum wage, barely meeting rent. We want to give our sons what our fathers gave us: lacrosse, three-car garages, summers on Cape Cod.

The frat boys are the right people, the ones who'll help us along. Two are sons of top financiers, two of doctors, three each of lawyers and congressmen. It's not just a brotherhood; it's a safety net, luminous protective filaments netting together to stop us from failing.

Without them, we might fall into the void.

Some girls are happy to head for the stairs. Others want to keep dancing, and some seem puzzled.

"What?" the blond keeps shouting at Westin, her face blank with confusion. "What did you say?"

We're annoyed. Don't they want to go to a quieter place, where we can actually get to know each other? Don't they want to have some fun? Beneath this lies another truth: We're unwilling, incapable, of letting these silly girls stand in our way.

Their tiny wrists are useless as instruments of self-defense. Our hands encircle them completely, and we tug them toward the stairs. The brunette giggles, looking as unsteady in her heels as a baby giraffe. She can barely walk on a flat surface, and the stairs prove much more treacherous. She's drunk, too, tripping all over herself, so we put our arms around her waist and help her climb.

"I wanna dance," the blond says. "Wanna—downstairs." She's slurring her words, stumbling against the wall, clinging to the stair railing. Westin grabs her arm and pulls her up the last three steps to the landing.

Upstairs, lights from outside come through the bedroom windows and spill into the hallway, striping the floor. This is where our brothers live. They've vacated the rooms to give us space for our quest. Even up here, we can hear the music, smell the alcohol and churning bodies.

A few of the doors are already closed, the most ambitious of our pledge group ahead of the game. From one room we hear a moan, and then the door flies open. Two of our fellow pledges come out, buttoning up their shirts and grinning.

Once, years ago, our mothers told us sex was only meaningful if we did it with someone we loved. Some people did it randomly, an empty and animal act, but she wanted us to wait. If we waited for love, it could be the best thing in life, the closest we would ever be to another person. We pretended to be grossed out when they cast meaningful glances at our fathers. Secretly, though, we thought it might be nice. We wondered if it would happen to us.

But now? Our mothers and fathers split up within two years of that little talk. One cheated on the other with a coworker. We know "true love" isn't real. It's a Disney concoction, a fairy tale dream, punctured by the sharp, cold spur of reality.

A girl who doesn't have sex on the first date is a prude. A guy who hasn't lost his virginity by nineteen is a sucker. If you feel like you're in love, it won't last. The scientists have discovered that biology gives "love" a four-year expiration date, just enough time to pop out a kid.

We yank the girls by their wrists and lead them to the rooms.

"How're we gonna do this?" Westin says. "How're we gonna split it up?" By now, we've realized we have two girls and four guys. The guys need to go in pairs so one can complete the task while the other documents. "Drew, how about you and me take Kate here?"

"My name's not Kate," the blond mutters, but no one listens to her.

Drew shakes his head, his face dark. He doesn't look drunk.

"No," he says. "She's wasted. It's not right."

"Come on, man, you're gonna worry about morals now, after what you did last weekend?" Westin says. "Just do it!"

"Do it!" the rest of us yell. Drew's reluctance scares us. It touches something inside us, in our secret hearts. If we watch him any longer, he might infect us.

"No," Drew says again. A beat passes where nothing happens. Then, to everyone's shock, he cries. We're silent, almost won over by his sorrow.

"Drew, you suck," one of us says. The harsh voice snatches our attention, reminds us to keep going.

We snap a picture of the tears staining his face just before he dashes down the stairs. We mock him in disgusted voices. He won't become one of us.

As we push the girls down onto the beds, we see in the light from the windows that the blond has a gap between her front teeth, the brunette a white puckered scar below her ear. But we can't stop for such details. These aren't girls with names, personalities, and quirks, but girls, plural—a cartoon, a commodity, here for our pleasure and consumption. They have spindly legs, weak, flailing arms, and high-pitched baby doll voices. Their dresses are so short and their push-up bras so tight beneath their breasts. Going out, wearing clothes like these? They knew this would happen.

For a moment, we wonder what this will do to us, to them. Maybe we're destroying the possibility love will ever descend on us. It might be like a pure white bird wheeling up high in the sky. It might decide to skip our polluted swamps in favor of places with green grass and fresh water. But we push that silly sadness out of our minds. This is life, where only the strongest can win. We determined long ago that we must be winners.

Our hands are on their chests to keep them down, but it's not necessary. The girls are quiet now, limp and welcoming. It's almost like they understand what we're doing. They know it's not our fault. Even though we want to, there is no way we can stop.

MABEL

That year, we kept Christmas a quiet affair. It used to be an opportunity to parade before the neighbors, stack up our family successes against the Dohertys' perpetual debt and the Millers' lackluster children. I had always been the ace, the one my mother could never be openly proud of in public because it would overwhelm their insecurities.

Now my name was in the papers, just as I'd always hoped. But while I understood in theory that with fame came controversy, I had never anticipated the vitriol I'd face over such a small thing, a thing that could be construed as a misunderstanding.

Young reporter shamed.

"Star" journalist accused of plagiarism.

Millions of books are published each year, thousands every hour. Why, then, should mine be the focus of their hatred? Their headlines were like paper cuts to my heart.

I still had two free days before my flight back to the West Coast, so I decided to peruse my old school diaries. More than a dozen volumes occupied space on the bookshelf in my old room, a detailed chronicle of my life from the ages of thirteen to twenty-two. I sat on the floor and chose one from the early days. I wanted to revisit a time when my ambitions hovered pleasantly within reach: awards at school, shorter times in the mile run, periodic recognition as student of the month.

Memory is a self-serving historian, enhancing the triumphant, easing the unflattering. I was pleased to discover I remembered the words that led to my victory in the school-wide spelling bee—vicissitude, pique, ratatouille. But I hadn't the faintest recollection of ruining a science lab by spilling acid on the table.

Nor did I recall how Mabel had given me my favorite collection of essays. I was shocked to read that it had been a gift for my thirteenth birthday. For years, I'd been convinced that I purchased the book myself.

In the back of the diary was a handmade card, a piece of printer paper folded in fourths, the message inside penned in perfect letters, as formal and impersonal as if it had been typewritten. Dearest Kate, Happy Birthday! Your Best Friend, Mabel. In each corner, she had drawn a staid five-pointed star. She must've used a ruler or a stencil to make all the points aligned, all the angles just right: a fragment of the perfection she always sought, but achieved only in small things.

A knock at my disturbed me.

"What is it?" I said.

"Someone's asking for you on the phone," came my mother's muffled voice. "I think it's a reporter."

"I told you to say I'm not here."

"Sorry."

I felt ashamed at the old teenage snappishness that crept into my voice. Just being in this room—with its blue carpet, single bed, and periwinkle walls—brought me back to the years when the intrusion of someone who cared was a thing to resent.

I went to the door to apologize, but my mother had already retreated downstairs.

I didn't have any particular feelings about Mabel, the other smartest girl in first grade, until I heard boys on the playground calling her "Big Bird." Mabel grew fast and early; she towered a foot over than everybody else. Gentle and awkward, she hung on the fringes of groups, saying nothing. Cruelty toward someone so harmless enraged me. I picked up a fistful of gravel and threw it at the perpetrators who ran, scowling.

Soon, I spent afternoons at Mabel's house. We built tiny stick villages in the mulch of her mother's shrub garden, complete with houses, paths, and town centers. We threw tennis balls to Mabel's two golden retrievers in the back yard. We always sat next to each other on the bus. Though we looked quite different—she, tall and dark-haired; I, short and fair—people often took us for sisters. That kind of closeness could only be explained by blood.

I could still picture her just as she was then: her oval glasses, her hair in a limp bun at her neck, her awkward stiffness, like she never quite knew where to put her feet and hands. She had two different-colored eyes, one blue and one green, the result of a cataracts surgery when she was two years old. The procedure had saved one eye but left the other blind.

We were best friends for seven years. Sometimes, even now, I dreamt about her. If jealousy and petty drama hadn't ruined things, maybe we would still be in touch. Maybe I would have someone to tell about my current crisis, about how success had finally gotten tired of me and walked away.

Mabel was a note-taker, a studier, the conscientious sort of student who pleases teachers best. I was a trouble-maker who found school too easy for me. It irritated and bored me, and I put in just enough effort to earn the highest average in each subject. Some teachers hated my fidgeting and negativity; they resented that I still managed to do well. Others called me brilliant, destined to do something that would shake the world.

I believed their immodest predictions. As a student, grades and intelligence were the only things that mattered. Economic factors, professional connections, sheer luck—those were for lesser minds; they would never touch me.

By eighth grade, I grew impatient with Mabel, as I did with all easy things in life. She joined the same clubs I did, read the same books, accompanied me to track, to church, to school. When I became determined to learn about fashion—a smart person could learn anything, after all—and shopped with my mother to buy new shirts in teal, emerald, and crimson, I hated when Mabel soon acquired the same colors. Why couldn't she be her own person, I railed in my diary. Why couldn't she leave me alone once in awhile, make her own choices, choose her own fate?

I told Mabel not to sit with me at lunch today. I wanted to sit with Elizabeth and Jessica and it wouldn't look good if she came along. She acted all dramatic about it, but why shouldn't I try to make new friends? Why should I be stuck with the same friend my whole life?

How easy it was to throw away the constant, the sure-won.

It all started with a little recycling. After my first book debuted to lukewarm praise and paltry sales, I found I had nothing to write. My "next book" seemed a chimera, even my next blog post. Would anyone notice if I reused a sentence here and there, repurposed a thesis or a clever phrase?

Was it really so wrong to write the same thing twice? Most of us repeat the same stories much more often than that. How many times had my parents told me how they met, married, survived their first jobs? So many that I knew these tales by heart, as if they were my own. Writers, too, circle the same worn narratives: love, war, time. Didn't one of the great American novelists build each of his stories around a particular sort of flapper, all joy and flirtation at eighteen, but madness and desolation at thirty-eight? We struggle so long to find those hard-won words. Once we discover them, how can anyone expect us to let them go?

It shouldn't have surprised me that Mabel would find someone else: the new girl in town, Kaycee, whom I hated for her poorly-spelled name. Her appearance struck me as somehow degenerate: greasy blond hair, red and white checkered shoes; band shirts; studded belts. With the uncanny instinct of a predator, she sensed the rift between Mabel and me and swooped in to take my place.

Now it wasn't I who roved elsewhere for lunch, but Mabel. She sat with Kaycee, and the two of them hunched over their sandwiches, giggling and darting significant glances in what might've been my direction.

Sometimes, as an adult, I told the story of our falling-out to ambitious women who I hoped might become my friends. Over cocktails after work, I offered up what had once been the core of my life as a trifling amusement. The story went like this: Mabel, jealous of my superior academic talent, had been looking for an excuse to dump me. When Kaycee showed up, with her makeup-ringed eyes and tales of woe about nothing, Mabel saw someone weak, and therefore more comfortable to be around. When I refused to like Kaycee, Mabel grew righteous and lofty. She pretended not to talk to me anymore because I was "mean"—but really because she couldn't stand that I was better.

How many times had I told this to myself, crowing inwardly about the past? It portrayed me as ambitious, uncompromising despite social pressure, the kind of woman I wanted to be.

"Sounds like someone needed to chill out," one said. She was a year younger than me, but she seemed so much older, with her sleek blond bob, expert eyeliner, and stark statement jewelry. She was a product designer at a start-up tech firm, and she had already filed several patents under her name.

"Yeah," I said, pleased that she agreed with my analysis.

It wasn't until later, when she became too busy to hang out, that I realized she might've been referring to me.

It was true that I sometimes went beyond the creative reuse of my work. There were sentences and phrases I'd read and loved so much that they felt like mine. The media called it "stealing," but I felt I was the victim. The other journalists stole words, snatched particular combinations out of air and set them down with an eternal stamp of ownership. This seemed to me harsh and unjust. What if the first men to reach the South Pole erected a fence and said no one else could visit? Words, to me, were like geographies: public things, consumed repeatedly to increase the world's delight.

I remembered nothing of the note Kaycee had given me until it fell from between the diary pages:

You act like I stole her, but all I did was be nice to her. Unlike you. You never call her anymore & you don't sit with her on the bus. You don't even know what she's been going through lately. So stop being mean and stop trying to ruin her life.

What had Mabel been going through? I couldn't remember anything besides her choice of Kaycee as a friend. There were rumors that Kaycee had an eating disorder, which I couldn't understand. Why would anyone starve herself to look like sexist pictures of women that were obviously Photoshopped?

Today Mabel sat with me for the first time in a while. She seemed upset, but I had to ask her several times before she said what was wrong. Turns out she's cutting herself. I was shocked. She wouldn't say exactly why but mumbled something about school and how she should be doing better and she feels the need to "punish" herself. I guess I should probably care, but I just feel annoyed. Why would she do such a dumb thing? She's as weak as I thought.

I'd recorded my actions so confidently in my neat print, blue ink marching across the page without a shadow of remorse. Everyone said thirteen-year-old girls were awful, but I'd always pinpointed this awfulness in others. Other people's crimes were much easier to recall.

I traded her secret like a bargaining chip, a signal to the alpha girls that I had finished with Mabel and her loser-ish ways. It wasn't long before Elizabeth and Jessica spread it around the whole school. Mabel grew infrequent in my diary, but no less vivid.

Somebody stuffed an envelope into Mabel's locker the other day. It had a razor and a note telling her to get it over with.

I sat on the floor and stared at the wall. Me, the heroine of my own tale, hardly as pure and spotless as I thought.

It was easy to infer that she might be home for Christmas, even easier to find her online. Her Facebook pictures were as dowdy as I'd suspected, her tweets formulaic and inoffensive. She was a software programmer. That alone negated my supposed advantages as valedictorian and Ivy League graduate. I was a lowly journalist. She definitely made more than me.

A few clicks led to a company email address where I wrote asking if she'd like to meet. Sure, she wrote back. I let her name the time and place.

———— ∿∿ ————

Her hair was pulled into a flat bun at her neck. She wore a droopy tan shirt with frayed black lace around the sleeves. She still had the same gray, oval glasses, behind which her eyes looked as weak and shielded as her mother's. I had worn my best: dark jeans, a new blazer, the sort of makeup that made your eyes look bigger without appearing to be makeup at all.

We sat at a table by the window of the cafe, looking out onto a parking lot with few cars.

"So, what are you up to these days?" I asked, as though I didn't already know—a social media pretense both necessary and hypocritical. Of course everyone looked at everyone else's pictures and posts. That was what they were for, all the choreographed selfies and sunsets and artfully swirled lattes.

"I'm programming for a start-up in Boston. A lot of hours, but it's really fun, and my coworkers are great." She smiled and leaned forward confidentially. "And the pay is fantastic. Much better than I thought I'd be doing, right out of school."

"Wow, good for you."

I tried to pass myself off as glamorous: roving reporter, articles in publications impressive for my age. But it felt like the fake sheen on costume jewelry, a gold that rubs off to reveal the cheap green underneath.

"So," I said, fiddling with my coffee cup. "So, I was thinking. It's too bad we fell out of touch."

She cocked her head to one side, a strangely graceful gesture in a person otherwise so ungainly. I expected her to say something, but she didn't. It struck me how accurate the name "Big Bird" had been.

"I've been thinking, maybe it was all my fault. And I'm really sorry." I glanced at her. She had to know what I meant.

It occurred to me to wonder if she knew about my scandal, my shame. I wondered if she loved the schadenfreude, if she felt vindicated by my fall.

"What was your fault?"

"Well, everything."

A news van pulled up outside.

"What do you mean?"

I stared out the window as a reporter got out and walked toward my car. I wondered how he knew it was mine, and how long it would take him to come into the store.

Across the table, I'd expected Mabel's face might be mocking, faking innocent, but instead she looked genuinely puzzled. She followed my eyes as they went back to the reporter, who now approached the door.

Her voice was quiet, understanding. "Do you need a ride? My car's in the back."

I followed her out the back of the coffee shop. We climbed into her new red BMW, sleek and shiny as a tube of lipstick. She waited for me to buckle my seatbelt before starting the ignition.

My greatest vanity was not my looks, not my CV, but this: thinking she befriended Kaycee just to spite me. Thinking what I did was important enough for her to remember.

THE WAY YOU COVER

Greg had watched Kayla for three months now, and he still didn't know which of her details he liked best. She had her hair tied up messily, her eyes lined in dark makeup. Her skin, smooth and creamy, reminded him of dairy products: whole milk, ice cream, brie.

The neck of her ukulele poked up from the bottom of the screen. She sat against the usual yellow wall, a blank wall that betrayed nothing about her. As she strummed the strings, he noticed her fingernails bore light blue nail polish.

Her voice got him every time. Usually high, sweet voices, voices that seemed to be pretending, irritated him, but hers was different. The way she furrowed her brows on the saddest words, the way she shook her head as she modulated up for the final chorus, how she laughed nervously as soon as a song ended, reaching up to shut off the webcam—all these details convinced him that, unlike everyone else, she was sincere.

After watching the song, he rewound to the spot at the beginning, the part where she bit the side of her lower lip. Other viewers had noticed, too. Their appreciation was recorded in the comments.

0:34: sexxxxyyyyy!

What had she been thinking—was she nervous, or did she realize how alluring it would look?

"Bye-e," she said, grinning and reaching up to shut off the camera.

Greg adjusted his pants and sighed. A hundred thousand views, maybe only fifty of them due to him. Thousands of other people watched her, maybe thousands of guys. He expanded the video to full screen, so he didn't see the number of plays. When she looked into her web cam, he pretended she was looking only at him.

<hr />

"Come on," Dylan said, holding the spray paint can out to Greg. "It's just a little payback for all those hours we wasted."

Greg shook his head. Dylan hadn't told him they'd driven to the cat shelter. He had no idea Greg actually liked it. Originally, it had been community service hours, but Greg realized he liked cats a lot more than people.

Dylan shook the can. A few weeks ago, when they'd discussed what to do before graduation, "something big," it had been a long string of disasters: running away after chalking gigantic dicks on prudish Amelia's driveway, tearing down the highway at ninety in Dylan's ancient Camry until the frame rattled. But this—Greg hated this.

He tossed his spray paint on the ground and walked away.

"Hey! Where are you going?"

Greg didn't answer. He shoved his hands in his pockets and started on the two-mile walk home, keeping on the grass at the edge of the road.

People were the reason Greg wanted to be a vet. He didn't mind when the cats hissed or scratched. They did it because they were scared, small and vulnerable. But when people did something bad, Greg always felt disappointed. Recently Dylan had almost been kicked out of the National Honor Society for plagiarizing an essay. Worse, the day before, driving both of them home from school, Dylan purposely sped up to hit a rabbit that ran into the road. When Greg thought about it, his stomach twisted into a knot of sick anger. In theory, people could reason and feel compassion, but from what Greg could see, they hardly ever used it.

Kalya was different, though. He felt sure of it. Back at home, he ran upstairs to his room. Sasha, one of his young tabby cats, sat in his desk chair.

"Hey, Sash," he said, petting her. She purred and arched up against his hand. Sasha was the friendliest of the three he'd adopted over the last year. His mom said he could adopt as many cats as he could pay for, not realizing how much money he'd saved from his newspaper job over the summer.

Greg clicked on Kayla's YouTube channel. She had not replied to his comment on the new video, asking if she'd be willing to talk to him on Gmail. Pages of new comments already buried his humble request. Perhaps she'd never seen it. He wanted to talk to her, but there didn't seem to be a non-creepy way to do it. He knew so little about her.

At first, he Googled hopelessly, not expecting to really find anything. "Kayla ukulele," he typed. He re-read the old Huffington Post article from a few months ago, and a Gawker post that gushed about the "cuteness" of her "Boyfriend" cover.

Then, on the third page of the search, Greg found a PDF of a high school newsletter posted a few days ago, titled SENIOR PROFILES. "Kayla Ponterry's first ukulele video went viral last year. Since then, she's gained millions of views on all her covers. She's a homegrown star!"

He searched for Lenfield Academy, Massachusetts. A public school with a fancy name. Greg then looked up "Ponterry" in the white pages and put the address into Google maps. A red teardrop marked her house. Of all the places in the world, Kayla lived in the town next door.

He still wanted to do something memorable before graduation, something big. This was it. He would meet her.

Kayla lived on a wide, silent street with houses blighted like rotten teeth: faded paint, crooked shutters, grass shooting through cracks in the crumbling driveways. Greg parked on the side of the street and rolled down his window. A yellow ranch house at the end of the bulb-shaped road, the wild lawn bordered by woods on one side and a rusted chain-link fence on the other, matched the address he'd found online. At the edge of the woods sat a battered red pick-up truck, its fender hanging down on one side. He stared. He'd always imagined her among topiary gardens and shining countertops, chlorinated pools and glass-doored showers. Maybe the address was wrong.

The sound of an instrument: high, sweet strumming, reaffirmed his quest from an open window on the second floor. Greg stopped breathing so he could listen. The chords sounded familiar. He gripped his sweaty car keys. It had to be her. Now, instead of the unbearable distance of a laptop screen, it was just a physical wall between them. He tried convincing himself to knock on the door. Maybe he'd say he was looking for a lost pet. But the music stopped, and a minute later, the front door opened. It was her.

"Shit," Greg whispered. She wore a short yellow dress and a cross-body black leather purse with fringes and metal studs. She skipped down the front steps and climbed into the pick-up truck. It growled as she started the ignition, and black smoke sputtered out of the exhaust pipe. She pulled over the lawn and drove away, leaving behind two trails of mangled grass.

Greg hadn't even seen her for thirty seconds, and now she was speeding away. He started the car. Up ahead, she took a turn down another road. He slammed on the gas to catch up.

Kayla turned into a neighborhood on the other side of town, a shallow cul-de-sac with a few houses around a wide circle of pavement and parked by the curb. Greg pulled into the driveway behind her and waited until she left her truck. Once she disappeared around the corner, he parked behind her truck and jogged in the direction she had gone, following her into the next neighborhood.

This street had houses three times the size of his and glittering black SUVs in every driveway. Kayla walked up to a house where people milled under white awnings, plastic cups in hand. She slowed and rested one hand on her purse as she traipsed across the grass. A girl with short hair waved at her, and together, they walked to the back of the house.

Greg hurried after them. Throngs of people covered the green expanse of the back yard. He threaded his way through the crowd, circling the yard four times, but didn't catch sight of Kayla. Maybe she'd left already. He paused near the bouncy castle and sighed. Everything felt ridiculous and pointless in that moment. Working so hard to go to community college. Following a girl he'd seen on YouTube only to end up alone at some stranger's party.

A bunch of kids squealed inside the castle, which jerked with their every jump. Enjoying the absurdity of his situation, Greg took his shoes off and threw them on the grass. He crawled through the front flap. Inside were six or seven kids, skinny as pencils, jumping as hard as they could. As he tried to stand up, he almost fell down, but he flapped his arms and regained balance. A little girl jumped over to him.

"Who are you?" she asked, poking a finger in his stomach.

"Greg," he said. "Who are you?" The girl giggled and jumped away.

Greg laughed. He started to jump. When he landed, his feet sank deep into the plastic, and the kids shrieked, trying not to fall into him. Soon, they were all laughing. With each jump, Greg soared upwards, his head crashing into the soft top of the castle. He had just started to forget his misery when, through the black mesh of the other side, he saw a girl in a yellow dress.

He bounded across in two leaps and bounced lightly near the side, pressing his face against the mesh. She bent over, rummaging in one of the coolers next to the castle. A black bag hung from her shoulder, and blonde hair hid her eyes. It was definitely Kayla. She took out what looked like a beer.

"Hey," Greg said. She did not respond. "Hey," he said, more loudly. But she turned away to pop off the top of the beer against a wooden post sticking up from the lawn.

A middle-aged woman glided over, her gray dress flowing around her like wisps of cloud.

"Hello, Kayla."

"Hey," Kayla said. She put one hand on her bag, and with the other, held the beer awkwardly.

"Dear, remind me how old you are?" the woman said, her voice smooth and poisonous.

"My parents let me."

"Well, this isn't exactly your parents' house, is it?" The woman looked around and laughed. "I'm not quite sure you could mistake the two."

"Bitch," Kayla muttered.

"Excuse me?" The woman's mouth became a round "O". Her plucked eyebrows looked like they were trying to leap off her face.

Kayla threw the beer down on the lawn where it spilled out in a frothy puddle. She then gripped her bag and strode away.

Greg scrambled over to the front flap and slid out of the castle. He grabbed his sneakers and ran after her, but she had already reached the side of the house.

"Hey, Kayla! Wait!" he said.

She turned around and looked at him, forehead wrinkled.

"Do I know you?"

"No," he said, his face feeling hot. "I saw what happened back there. I heard her say your name."

"Oh, her." She slowed and walked next to him.

"Who is she?"

"My friend's mom, Mrs. Mason. This is their fabulous, ancestral home." She swept an arm grandly and smirked. "That bitch hates me."

Her golden hair shone in the sun; she wore dark makeup and fake lashes, accentuating her blue eyes.

"How could anyone hate you?" Greg blurted.

Kayla smiled and looked at him. Her eyes felt like a hot light on his face. "Aren't you sweet." She shrugged. "'Cause she thinks I'm from a trailer park. Thinks I'm corrupting sweet Natalie or something because I took her tanning. God, if they find out, they might kick her out of Tufts."

"She's going to Tufts? That's so unfair." Greg's voice was vehement on both of their behalves. Of course a girl who lived in a house like this could afford to go.

"Exactly. What she doesn't know is, Natalie's the one who begged to go tanning in the first place." Kayla swung her arms around, spinning her bag. "Want to see it? The ancestral home?"

"Sure." Pleasure flooded Greg, almost as much as when he'd won the PETA essay contest last year.

Greg followed Kayla inside. A burgundy shag carpet led down the hallway into a sunlit kitchen. "Where's your friend?"

"Had to get makeup done for prom. Can't do it herself, apparently." Kayla glanced into the kitchen. "Everyone's outside. Come on." She ran up the two-flight staircase, sliding her hand along the gleaming banister. Greg ran after her, wondering if Mrs. Mason had seen them.

"Are you sure we should—"

"Relax. I've been here a million times." She opened a door. "This is Natalie's room." A canopy bed, covered with sheer white drapes, dominated the center of the room. "It's a water bed," Kayla said, sitting down and leaning back on her arms. She patted the space next to her. Greg hesitated.

"Come on, it's not like a guy's never been on it before."

Greg sat down, struggling to keep his back straight. Kayla looked at him. "What's your name, anyway?"

"Greg."

"I'm Kayla. Although I guess you already knew that."

He tried to look at her without looking at her, but it might appear strange to peer at her sideways, so he chose a neutral spot on the floor instead.

"So, what are your hopes and dreams?"

"What?" Greg said, laughing.

"I know it's weird, but it's my ice breaker. I ask everyone. So tell me." She look at him with wide eyes.

"Well... I've always wanted to go to Tufts. I got in, but it's way too expensive. Hell, even UMass is too expensive. So I'm going to Bristol Community College instead." He twisted his mouth as he said it. The words tumbled from him, easier to say than he'd imagined. Maybe it was her.

Kayla frowned. "That sucks."

Silence fell between them, and Greg wondered how to bring up music. He wanted her to talk about it, but it would seem too contrived. Instead, he said, "This is kind of recent, but I've been thinking about becoming a vet."

"Aw, I love animals!"

"Yeah, lately I've been thinking how great it would be to help animals get better."

"Oh, you should meet the cat. This'll be the first test of your vetting skills." Kayla sprang off the bed, brushing against his arm.

Greg laughed. "You're adventurous."

"She's usually in Mrs. Mason's room," Kayla said, tiptoeing down the hall. "Come on," she whispered.

Mrs. Mason's bedroom sported the biggest bed Greg had ever seen. The hardwood floors shone like the surface of a mirror, and the matching oak furniture stood in contrast to the dark floor. The bed had four wooden banisters with gold inlay and a red canopy hanging above. A congested wheeze came from the fancy pillow in the middle of the bed. Greg looked again and realized it was actually a cat—one of the expensive purebred ones, with blue eyes and the face pushed in. The cat looked at them with disdain.

Kayla giggled. "Meet Fabiola. Careful there. She looks dumb, but she's vicious."

"Fabiola?"

"Only the Masons," Kayla said, shaking her head.

Greg approached the bed, and Fabiola pricked her ears toward him. He paused so she wouldn't feel threatened. Meanwhile, Kayla walked around the room, inspecting the furniture. She pointed to something on the nightstand behind him and laughed. Greg looked over and saw the object of her derision: a crystal sculpture of a cat, tail erect and head lifted high, as though intended to appear noble. Greg laughed too, and Kayla caught his eye.

"You never said what your hopes and dreams are," he said.

"That's 'cause I don't have any." She touched the edge of the bedspread. Fabiola narrowed her eyes. "You should feel this, it's like, silk or something." Greg touchd it. Fabiola hissed, showing her needle-sharp teeth.

"Whoa," he said, drawing back. Kayla laughed.

"Come on," Greg said. "I'm sure you have some hopes."

She looked out the window and put her hand on her bag. "I wanted to go to Berklee. The music school."

"What happened?"

"Same as you. Got in, can't afford it. So it's community college for me." She went over to the bureau. "This is insane," she said, holding up a glittering necklace. "I think it might be real diamonds."

"What do you play?"

"I sing. And play piano, guitar, and ukulele." She fingered the necklace. "I could totally steal this and sell it to pay for college. But the bitch probably has a GPS on it." She put it down.

"I bet you're really good at singing."

"I'm okay."

"Maybe I can hear you sometime. Sing, I mean."

She looked at him from the corner of her eye. "So you do wanna see me again?"

"I wouldn't mind it."

"Maybe we can arrange that."

Greg wanted to shout and pump his fist in the air, but instead, he took another step toward Fabiola. If he could convince the cat to like him, it might impress Kayla.

He edged forward slowly, holding out his hand while Kayla watched. Fabiola stared at him, looking offended. He froze. Her nostrils flared slightly, like she was trying to catch his scent, so he moved his hand imperceptibly closer. She stretched forward and sniffed at his hand. That seemed to satisfy her. Gently, Greg reached forward and stroked the back of her head. She stiffened at first, but then relaxed, closed her eyes, and purred.

"Wow, good job," Kayla said. "That cat's never liked anyone besides Mrs. Mason."

Greg felt pleased. He really did have a knack with animals. "Good cat, Fabi. Nice kitty."

One of the cat's ears twitched. Suddenly, she drew back, hissed, and scratched Greg's hand.

"Shit!" Greg jumped back. He smashed into the nightstand behind him and heard a crash. He turned to see a million splinters of glass all over the hardwood floor.

"Run!" Kayla said. They dashed out of the room and down the stairs. They walked quickly across the front lawn until they were past the line of cars. At the end of the neighborhood, Kayla started running again, and Greg ran with her.

The sting of the three red scratches on his hand didn't distract him from the realization that he was running with Kayla, and that they were laughing like good friends as they approached their cars. He imagined them together. She'd play ukulele for him and sing for him alone. Maybe she'd let him touch her hair. Maybe he would even get to kiss her.

Kayla giggled as they came to a stop, her hair messy after running with flyaways going every which direction. "That was hilarious," she gasped. "I wish I could see the look on her face when she sees that stupid statue."

"Yeah."

"Hey." She poked him with her elbow. "Want to hang out at my place?"

His legs felt weak. He'd imagined it would be the other way around, but here she was surprising him again, preempting his asking.

"Sure."

"Oh, shoot! Was your car back on that other street? I wasn't thinking when we ran."

"No, it's right there," Greg said, pointing. "Behind yours." He thought the beat-up cars looked good together. Two of a kind.

Kayla stared at him. "How did you know that's my car?"

Greg felt like a black hole had opened up in his stomach.

"I just figured. Since we ran all the way here, and that one's mine, and process of elimination."

"Why'd you park over here?"

"You know." He shrugged unconvincingly. "Shitty old car, didn't want them to see it."

She crossed her arms. "Were you following me?"

"No!" Greg said. "Why would I follow you?"

She stared at him. "Have you seen my videos?"

"What videos?"

"Liar. Have you been stalking me for like, months?"

"No," Greg said. "Only today."

"Oh, only today. That makes it better."

"No, that's not what I meant. I just really wanted to meet you, you're amazing—"

"God, what a creep. I was actually starting to like you."

"I just wanted to meet you." Greg felt the small, fragile hope in his chest shatter as he spoke the words.

"So you couldn't do it in a more normal way, like, message me or something?"

"I tried to, but you never replied."

She snorted. "Yeah, because everyone who messages me is probably like a rapist or something."

"Oh, so that would have gone so much better for me, if that's what you think. God, I just wanted to get to know you," Greg said. "Is that so horribly evil?"

"How did you follow me?"

"I went to your house. I was gonna knock on the door or something, but then you started driving, so I panicked and followed you."

She frowned. "That might be kind of cute, if only it weren't so creepy."

"I swear, I just—"

"Isn't that what all the murders say?"

"Come on, you honestly think I'm gonna murder you?"

"Never know. You did stalk me on the Internet, find out where I live, and follow me to a party."

"Come on, Kayla, I—"

"I'm gonna drive away, and you better not follow me, or I'm calling the police. Got it?"

"Geez, okay."

She unlocked her door manually and got in the car. He expected her to flip him off as she drove away, but she didn't. She just looked at him out the window and stepped on the gas.

Graduation was lame. He had to listen to Julie Jackson, who'd beaten him for valedictorian by hundredths of a point, talk about how great high school was, and then he had to watch three hundred kids walk across the stage. It seemed like everyone except him had air-horn wielding fans, Frisbee-catching pranks, and friends to hug at the "kiss and cry" robe return.

An empty summer languished before him. He had little to do besides watch movies, mow his neighbor's lawn, and attempt to play the guitar he bought on eBay. When UPS dropped the box off at his door, he leapt up from his laptop to get it. He slit the tape and lifted the styrofoam packing sheet. The yellow wood of the instrument gleamed in the light, and when he brushed his thumb against the strings, they hummed. He imagined playing melancholy songs in his room. He'd leave the window open so anyone passing outside would know how much he'd lost. But despite all the instructional videos on YouTube, he couldn't make even the easiest chord sound right.

Instead, he watched Kayla's new video, a cover of "You Belong With Me," posted a week after graduation. "Hey, guys," she said, with distressingly sunny smile. She wore a green T-shirt and her usual dark makeup. She closed her eyes and shook her head as she sang the chorus: "Have you ever thought just maybe—you belong with me?"

Greg smacked his hand on his desk.

"Of course I've thought that!" he said. Greg frowned and clicked away vehemently. But after a few minutes of skimming through junk Gmail, he watched the video again. He felt like he'd been turned inside-out and his guts had sunburned, but it was no use looking away. Her image had been seared into his mind. Wherever he turned, he saw her wide eyes, her irreverent smile, her white skin, smooth and pale like brie.

Greg watched the video so many times that it appeared as a suggested page when he opened a new tab in his browser. He leaned back in his rolling chair and slammed his fist into the wall. Even if he couldn't see her in person, he wanted her to be happy. She was better than all the awful pop stars on the radio. She deserved to go to music school.

He remembered receiving an email once about a fundraiser, some site where you could donate to a breast cancer walk-a-thon. "Gofundme.com." He went to the site and read the instructions. It sounded simple enough.

His fingers rattled across the keyboard as he created the event: SEND THIS GIRL TO BERKLEE. Kayla is an amazing 18-year-old musician whose dream is to go to Berklee. She got accepted, but can't pay the tuition. If you love music, and want to see her as a big star someday, please help! Goal: $50,000. He laughed as he typed the number. Most projects on the site asked for only a few thousand dollars. It was a ridiculous goal.

He embedded her four best videos. From Google, he saved her most heart-stopping picture: a selfie taken from above, Kayla smiling up at the camera, her eyes bright against the black makeup, her cheek pressed against the neck of her ukulele.

Skimming over his work, Greg frowned. Of all the thousands of pages, it was unlikely anyone would donate to his. But it couldn't hurt to try. He posted the link on his Facebook page and on each one of her YouTube videos, then went to sleep.

Someone posted the link on Kayla's Facebook fan page; others posted it on Twitter. Thousands of people donated with credit cards and PayPal accounts, some as little as two dollars, others up to fifty or a hundred. Hardly thirty days had passed, and Greg could barely believe that he had reached $51,250.92, almost enough to send her to college for a year. Once the money arrived in his bank account, he wrote a check for $51,350.00, adding in a hundred dollars he had left over from the summer. He added a sticky note. "College tuition, courtesy of Gofundme.com. Maybe it's still not too late to accept the offer? —G"

Greg put it in a thick yellow envelope and drove to her house. His knees felt weak as he crossed the lawn to her stoop. Had she told her parents about him? Would she call the police? He rang the bell and waited, straining to hear anything. But none of them were home. He stuck the envelope in the door and left, almost relieved no one had answered.

He found out the result from her Facebook fan page. One of her friends had posted an announcement: "Kayla's going to BERKLEE! Thanks everyone for all your support!" Greg swore when he saw it. They seemed intent on taking the credit for themselves.

A few days later, he got a text

hey greg its kayla. sorry i didnt text earlier. wanted 2 say thanks. should have sooner but it seemed so unreal... wanted to make sure it was real 1st... now im going 2 berklee 4 real! All thanks 2 u.

Sitting at his desk, Greg stared at his phone, double-checking to make sure the text was real. He resisted the urged to text back right away. He made himself wait a few minutes before replying. *howd u get this #?*

She texted back immediately. *google.*

He grinned. She had actually bothered to look him

up. *Creeper,* he texted back.

learned it from u... think ur kinda obsessed w me, 2 do that.

well guess it don't bother u. u looked pretty happy in ur last vid.

so u have been stalking. ur weird greg, kinda creepy, kinda sweet. anyway u think i never fake it in vids?

it was fake happy?

maybe...well i wanna take u out 4 coffee to say thanks. in a public place where u cant kidnap me.

dunno, not sure if i should trust u.

well u shud bc im awesome. and ur the stalker not me.

maybe i can take a risk. today? 5:00, starbucks on main st
k.

:)

Greg stared at his phone, warm in his hand, the screen still lit. He hurried back to his room to get ready.

PRESUMED CONSENT

R obert looked at Kristen before her solo. To prove she was ready, she stared straight back. She spent hours practicing: holding each note with a tuner and metronome, performing the whole thing a hundred times before the mirror, so that even if the light shone in her eyes, sheer muscle memory would sustain her without accidents. But it was the highest measure of her devotion that she produced a calm embouchure when she wanted to smile—that she managed, facing him, somehow still to breathe.

Her sound glittered golden in the cavernous dark hall. She marveled at how music arose from such mundane bodily mechanics: movements of the diaphragm, lungs, fingers, lips. Only after her final dangerous note passed did she allow herself to stare at him, his arms sweeping over the orchestra like a predatory bird taking flight. He had a day's worth of stubble on his sharp jaw; a baton-inflicted neck scar; a rough left hand, unclaimed by any woman's ring.

After the concert, Robert came down to the green room to pat backs and pinch cheeks. Sweat soaked through his shirt, his face exhausted and faintly tinged with gray. He tugged her short blond ponytail and said, "Good job, flute." She wished he'd touched something besides her hair so she would know the texture of his skin. She wondered what it would be like to hear him say her name.

———◦◦◦———

"Maybe I should major in music." Kristen tugged an unraveling string from the outside of her ancient flute case. Her penchant for music history was, admittedly, a recent development, but she considered Mozart's G-minor Symphony a perfect work of art, more worthy of study than wars or diabetes.

"Yeah, if you want to rot jobless with all the other poets and artists," Mary said. Kristen's roommate was a violist and economics major: depressingly practical. "How will you compete with people who went to actual music schools like Juilliard? Isn't it kind of late to switch majors?"

"Robert started conducting when he was a junior in college."

"So that's what this is about." Mary grinned. "You've heard, haven't you? He left the last place after an affair with a student. He's a player."

Of course Kristen knew the rumors. After one jilted student came forward, three others had tattled about champagne after rehearsal, dinners in penthouse restaurants, overnight visits to apartments stocked with tulips and down comforters. But all men were players, Kristen thought, until they met the right woman.

———◦◦◦———

Robert sat with his arms behind his head, feet kicked up and crossed on his desk. "So you're in my class, too? How come you never say anything?"

Kristen shrugged. She always sat in the back corner of the lecture hall, determined, until now, to repress the desire to know him. But now that she'd finally come to office hours—the excuse to ask why The Well-Tempered Clavier was well-tempered—she found herself unable to speak.

"So quiet," he said, leaning forward to smile at her. "Quiet, but good. I was impressed with your solo at the concert. Flute, what's your name?"

"Kristen."

"Kristen," he repeated. He said it even better than she had imagined: tuneful, a falling minor third. "I knew a girl with the same name, back when I played the oboe. Before I realized instruments were too hard and switched to conducting. You kids"—Kristen's stomach sank on the word kids—"I don't know how you do it."

What would she have done if she were a different girl, confident in her attractions? Would she wear a V-neck sweater, slap on thick makeup like paint? But all Kristen did was nod, nod, nod, like she wasn't curious about his life: how he got to study in London and Vienna; if the women he'd known were like she imagined, opera stars in crimson gowns, with ivory necks that betrayed the marks of his teeth.

Instead, she said, "I signed up for your Verdi seminar next semester."

"Ah, I hate to tell you." He leaned back in his chair, looking into the far corner of the room. "I suppose they haven't updated the course catalog. I won't be teaching. Don't worry, the course will still run, just with someone else."

"Why?"

"Health reasons. I have—never mind. It doesn't matter."

"Cancer?" she blurted out. It was the worst she could imagine, the most terrifying thing that could strike a man in his thirties.

"No, a kidney thing. It was so sudden. There was this—weakness, and I felt so tired and strange. Now they're saying I have to go on dialysis, almost immediately. Apparently, they filter all your blood through a machine and clean it for you. Charming."

"Can't you get a transplant?"

"Perhaps. The wait list is years long."

"Years?" Her trembled in its upper register; she hated that she could never control it as well as the flute.

He waved his hand. "Oh, don't look so stricken, darling, I'm only dying. It happens to everyone, you know."

Kristen felt as though the sky had been punctured; what appeared so solid and immutable now sagged, leaking light and air. She'd thought of Robert as a work of art, as enduring as a Beethoven symphony. But really, he was a bag of blood and bones, a delicate organism crawling across the surface of the earth. He could be broken so easily. He could fall, his brain pressing ardently to the sides of his skull; an errant vehicle could crush him, his blood painting the road; tumors could sprout like eager mushrooms on his insides, rotting his body from within. His mortality offended her, his life threatened by something so trivial as a kidney.

Kristen imagined the kidney as a bright red bean, some cartoon organ on a health poster. All because of this disobedient piece of flesh, lines creased his forehead, and gray roots sprouted in his hair. He eroded, and one day he would cease—but she refused to accept that. For certainly, in this age of modern medicine, the inevitable could be postponed.

Kidney donors, she read, were a rare and wanted lot. Only a fifth of dialysis patients were rescued each year; thousands of them died waiting. Some of them chose to die, tired of dependency on needles and machines. Once a donor was secured, however, the operation was simple and safe—a few small incisions, a little rest afterward, and it was like it had never happened. Some people even donated to complete strangers. They said it made them happy, knowing they'd saved someone's life.

Kristen cornered him just as he locked his office, inducing him to ask her to dessert. At the ritzy corner pastry shop she had never been to, he ordered cheesecake covered with fruit, cannoli, crème brulee, and espresso with whipped cream on top.

"I don't know what we're celebrating," he said, cutting a tart in half to share. "But it feels like a celebration, doesn't it? Enjoy things while you can."

"You can't find a donor?"

He laughed. "I don't have much in the way of family. Parents died in a car crash. My sister and I are estranged. And it's not like I can go around asking friends. It would feel wrong." He glanced at her quickly, as though to evaluate the effect of his statement.

The thing she had been planning bubbled up in her throat. "What about me?" she asked.

"What about you?" His eyebrows came together, seemingly puzzled about what she meant.

"I'm healthy. I only need one."

"Kristen," he laughed. "Be serious. You hardly know me."

"So?"

"That would hardly be—" But he couldn't seem to say the word appropriate.

"Just think about it." With poise she rarely found in his presence, she clinked her espresso cup against his.

———※———

Robert's email later that night expressed awe and confusion, asking to discuss further what she had said. Kristen smiled. The objective fact was that his life was worth saving. Each of his classes contained at least a hundred students; a hundred more participated in his orchestra. To all of them, he was the embodiment of art and culture, the beauty and rebellion of things they weren't supposed to waste time learning about. Because of him, she had learned Brahms's Fourth Symphony.

Because of him, she listened the sounds in her world. She noticed the way rain glistened on the red berry tree and the way the moon bled into the sky on hazy nights. So why shouldn't she do it? It was perfectly reasonable.

There was, of course, the nearly subliminal thought that no other woman would do this, not even Robert's own sister—that she would show him the depth of her feelings much better than she could with worshipful words or satin underwear. But those things didn't matter; the virtuous weight of her public reasons canceled them out.

———

They ate gnocchi in white wine sauce, trout baked with lemon, chocolate ganache for dessert.

"Kristen, I don't think it's right. To take that from a young girl like you—I can't do it."

"But that's the point. I'm young. I'll recover quickly. Please, there's no one I'd rather give it to than you."

He considered her. She could read in his face that he never expected this. Perhaps girls had stalked his office hours, sent him cards, shown up in trench coats at his apartment door—but none of them would have been capable of this.

Robert wanted to get to know her first, to decide if he could really do such a thing. Most of the time, they didn't talk about kidneys. He took her to the symphony, walking on the river, to dinner in the city, even to Lincoln Center in New York City for a production of La Traviata. After the opera, they went for champagne in a dark restaurant far up in a skyscraper.

"When are you going to say yes?" she asked. "I want to save you."

"So that's your motive."

"Everything would be awful without you." To her embarrassment, a few tears leaked onto her cheeks. He was instantly grave, dabbing at her with fatherly concern.

"You know, Kristen," he said, "you're not like the other girls. I can't imagine any one of them doing this."

"How many are there?"

"There were three. But none now, besides you."

"Only three?" He nodded.

"Don't believe me?" He sat down next to her. "All of this is worth it. The being sick, the dialysis, just to know you."

"Really?"

Instead of answering, he put his hand over hers and put his face near her cheek. But then he drew back. "No," he said, almost to himself. "You're too young."

She didn't worry. She was sure that, soon enough, he would change his mind.

The surgeon, pressing his thin lips together, demanded to know how old she was.

"Twenty-one." The number fell defiantly into the cold white room. In the hospital, the scent of mortality hung close, making her only more sure than before.

"Do you have parental permission?"

"I don't need it. I'm a legal adult."

Robert coughed and stood up from the chair where he'd been sitting. "If you deny a desperate patient care, aren't you liable? Aren't you liable if a patient dies because you stopped a perfectly acceptable donation?"

The surgeon wanted to speak to Kristen alone. "How well do you know this man?" he asked. "What about your family? Later on, one of them might need a donation."

Kristen hated what he said, this implication that genetic connection was the only sort that mattered among humans. She stared at him with disdain. "Don't question me. I'm doing it."

———～～———

A week later, on the surgery table, Kristen breathed in and out. She felt nervous enough to vomit up the kidney;

perhaps they could skip the surgery entirely. She'd never imagined she could feel her kidneys before, but now she thought she could sense them—two stones hanging toward her back, balancing each other, both slippery, red, small enough to fit in a hand.

The sharp scent of alcohol, a cool press at her side. A rub and a prick. As her head became grew heavy and her eyelids drooped down, she thought she saw a tree. On it hung kidneys large and small, glistening like fruit without the skin. A long line of people snaked up to the tree, waiting for their chance to pick one. The man in front of Kristen took two. "Most people don't know this," he whispered, "but kidneys function best in pairs, like eyes."

The scar on her stomach was small, a red trail the size of her index finger. It amazed her that an entire organ could have come out of it. She traced it again and again with the tip of one finger. It was just what she had wanted—a stamp on her flesh to prove her love.

Kristen slept with the shades open, so she could feel the sun as she curled up in her down comforter. She imagined the feeling was similar to when women had given birth. A dull, happy ache—the life of a person she loved, owed entirely to her. She expected to hear from him soon.

Days passed, a week. Ten days after the surgery, Kristen had still heard nothing. Perhaps there had been some complication with his surgery. Perhaps he was ill. He might be dying without her knowledge, withering away alone.

She called the hospital. She called him. She called the university music department; they knew nothing of his status. Images of crypts filled her mind: dank passages, a lone torch, stone effigies of ancient knights crowding his modest tomb. At last, there came an email, three sentences and nothing more:

I'm recovering slowly but nicely. Lying low for a while. Hope you are well.

Kristen sighed and sank into her sheets. It wasn't as much regard as she wanted, but soon, she was sure, she would hear more.

Pictures started appearing on social media. While Kristen struggled through the Verdi seminar, learning only how little she knew knew of opera and Roman numeral analysis, Robert lingered on some tropical island with turquoise oceans and sand as bright as the sun. He looked thinner than before, but his skin had darkened and his smile hadn't diminished. He took pictures of himself on the beach, in the jungle; he even shared a blurry photo of himself in a bioluminescent bay.

Most of the pictures were of women. Many women, hordes of them, a different one in every shot. Black women, white women, women of shades in between, all with lustrous hair and statuesque bodies in jewel-toned bikinis. His arm rested on their shoulders, curled around their waists. They smiled and kissed him on the cheek. The showiness of it could mean it was nothing—or just the opposite.

When Robert returned to campus, she spotted him on the street, whistling and wearing a fedora she'd never seen before. Kristen followed him into a coffee shop and stood silently behind him while he ordered his drink and stepped to the side. While he waited by the counter, she spoke. "Robert."

He turned around, startled. It surprised her that he smiled.

"Kristen. How are you doing?" She'd forgotten how wonderful his voice was. It implied melodies, notes rising and falling like birds that flew into the sky and circled before landing.

"So you were in the Caribbeans. Living it up."

"Yes, I was." He put his hands into his pockets, a satisfied gesture. "It was beautiful. You should go sometime, if you can."

"You were in the Caribbeans while I was lying in bed. Recovering from the surgery I underwent, to save you."

"Kristen, thanks for that. I can never thank you enough," Robert said. His eyes wandered from her to the corner of the shop, where a thin blond woman with numerous bangles on her wrists drank coffee alone.

"Who were the women in your pictures?"

"Excuse me?"

She stared at him. "Who are they?"

"That is, quite frankly, none of your business."

It is my business, Kristen thought. All of it is. All of it.

"I see," Robert said quietly. "You think just because you saved me, now you own my life? That I owe everything to you? Well."

"Robert?" the barista called, and Robert stepped forward to claim his drink.

"Good-bye," Robert said. Kristen grabbed his sleeve. He yanked it out of her hand, nodded calmly, and kept walking.

Over the next few months, Kristen started to believe she could feel the presence of her right kidney and the absence of her left. The remaining kidney felt like a smooth, heavy stone. It dangled precariously among her organs, ready to come loose at any moment now that she had cut its counterweight free.

Where the left kidney had been, she felt a hole—a hollow avoided by the other organs, as though they awaited its return. Sometimes, she dreamed she had kept her kidney in her purse, only to set the bag down and forget it. She lost her kidney on tables at cafeterias, on the counters of public bathrooms, in doctor's offices, in parks. She jolted awake and put her hand to her back, feeling the void. She should've been wiser; the slippery palm-sized treasure should've been hers alone.

Sometimes, Kristen closed her eyes and focused, trying to re-establish contact. If wounded veterans still felt the ghosts of their limbs, surely she could sense her own living organ. Sometimes, she thought she felt it moving—traveling inside the stranger's body, trapped against its will. If she concentrated, she could sense its shape in the dark. Her skin became warm and wet; around her, she could see the other organs pulsing and glistening in this dim inner cavern. It didn't matter where her kidney roamed; it would always be hers. She was like its mother. It was like her eye.

MAN AND MACHINE

The higher-ups corralled the deactivated robots upright in cages. I navigated the rows under the red light, searching for the only face that mattered. There, in the back. Her attractive features stood out; the other robots had been designed ugly on purpose.

"Rosalind," I whispered, foolishly expecting a response. Only my breath and the soft whine of the lights replied, no more of her pleasant hum, reassuring as a heartbeat. Rosalind was gone, her memory chip wiped clean.

Even in deactivation, her face held that mysterious semi-smile. I realized it was her default expression—not, as I had believed, a smile just for me.

I met Rosalind the week after the terrorists fled, when the city still gleamed with blood and broken glass. The commander introduced the robots to our unit. The robot cohort contained individuals who represented both genders and all races, their faces uniformly misshapen— eyes too close together, odd-shaped noses, warts.

"You'll use these robots for inspecting buildings abandoned by the terrorists," he said. "Their exteroceptive sensors can detect the vapors of eight different explosives, as well as chemical weapons like nerve agents. This way, we don't risk human lives."

He assigned each soldier a robot. By the time he reached me, they'd all been deployed. The commander took me aside. "There's one extra robot from the previous generation. Not an ideal model, but they're too expensive to waste. We thought you could handle it."

He led me into another room. The robot wore jeans and a V-neck and had skin the color of a coffee-flavored soy drink. Her eyes, large and green, followed me.

"This is RL38501X. We ordered humanoid robots after studies showed soldiers worked best with machines they related to. But this generation was too relatable. People got attached. Last year, a man followed his robot inside a booby-trapped building and died."

The robot smiled at me. Her kind expression reminded me of my mother, who had been killed with the rest of my family in the bombing of '32.

"It's just a machine," he said. "Think of it as it."

———— ∿∿ ————

As I directed the SmartCar to the edge of the city, RL38501X made conversation from her hermetically sealed compartment in the back.

"Are you from this area?" she asked.

"Nope. Transferred here to join the military back in '33."

"Do you like it?"

I shrugged. "Sometimes it's lonely."

"That is sad. No one should feel lonely."

I let her out at the checkpoint. It, I reminded myself. Its job was to investigate a suspected storage facility for Novichok agent powders. As I waited, I found myself hoping she would be safe. Be safe, RL... Who could remember that serial number? RL should signify a name, I decided. Rosalind.

While other robots were destroyed in explosions or contaminated by toxins, Rosalind went months without incident, and we were transferred closer to the battlefront. On our first anniversary, I drove her to the hill above the new city. We looked out over the scarred buildings, the roads strewn with litter and wreckage. In the morning light, if you forgot what it meant, the glittering debris almost looked beautiful.

"Your hand is like mine," Rosalind said. I wondered when she'd notice. My left hand was also a prosthesis. I had the same thin line on my wrist as she, the same titanium joints beneath artificial skin.

"I lost my real hand in an accident." Fleeing my besieged hometown, I fell in the road. An errant SmartCar crushed my hand.

Rosalind furrowed her eyebrows. "What is a 'real hand'? Is this not real?"

She touched my prosthesis. A static shock passed between us, sharp and bright, much more vivid than the faint sensations I was used to.

"Ow!" I felt guilty as soon as her face assumed a hurt expression. I grabbed her right hand with my left. She smiled. Quietly, we watched the sun rise over the city.

The squat concrete building Rosalind had to inspect that week unnerved me. Its broken windows gaped like missing teeth in the grin of some delinquent.

As I waited, I thought about where I'd take her that night. I had been checking her out of the robot storage room a couple nights a week, using maintenance as an excuse. We listened to music together. At first it confused her, but the last time, she'd seemed to enjoy it.

I stared out the windshield, wondering when she would return. It had been longer than usual. A call came in on my earpiece.

"Your robot has been contaminated. Return to base immediately."

"Contaminated? How?"

"A new strain of bacteria engineered by the terrorists. Extremely antibiotic resistant."

"But I can't just—"

"Return to base immediately. Your robot will be sent to BioLabs for analysis and disposed of safely. You'll be assigned a new one tomorrow."

The disposal facility was five miles from base, but adrenaline made it feel closer. I snuck into the basement and found her crammed in a cage like trash. I reached through the bars and took her dangling hand, drawing it toward me. Her silicone skin was perfect, poreless, cold.

With my right hand, I unscrewed my left prosthesis and dropped it on the floor. I unscrewed her left hand and attached it to my stump. As I walked away, my breath came shorter. Did I feel an itching in my chest, a dizziness? Would they find my body pockmarked and ridden with buboes? I didn't care. Without Rosalind, I was an orphan in this world.

INCOMPATIBLE
TRUTHS

Dance!" Keller Greene shouted. "Dance like it's your last minute to live!" Students laughed and swirled, flickering around him like flames. He'd pushed the desks to the walls so his class could imagine a haunted ballroom: crimson carpet, shining chandelier, scent of death. Two girls held hands and spun until one staggered, hitting her knee against a desk. Keller grinned. He wanted them to lose control. He wanted them to feel this exuberance, this riotous warmth, this ability to keep despair at bay.

Last night, the shed had gone up easily after the flare and hiss of the starter paper, the red glow spreading at its edges. The first flames stumbled uncertainly, but soon they grew strong, roaring orange mouths that devoured wood into ash. Keller wasn't trapped in this windowless classroom. If he closed his eyes, he could pretend the faint musk of the walls turning to smoke, soft gray tendrils curling from the tip of his match.

"Now!" Keller said, holding up an arm. "Enter—the Red Death!" He pointed to the boy crouching behind his desk. The boy sprang out and ran toward a group of girls near the door. The lights went out; girls squealed as the classroom fell black.

This darkness reminded him of the shed, with its birdseed fragrance and grimy windows. It was a mile from his own home on Smith's retired farm, so far buried in the wooded backyard the old man couldn't see Keller slip in, kneel, and cup his hands around an orange glow.

The classroom lights struggled back on. The period was nearly over, just as the enactment had exhausted its fuel.

"All right, everyone. Back to your desks." The fire had made the front page. In this small town, it was the most thrilling event in weeks. They had a picture of soggy black ash on the ground; hosing down the embers had been all the firefighters could do. Keller looked out at his class's smooth, trusting faces. What would they think if they knew?

But it didn't matter; they wouldn't find out. He was careful now. He'd purchased his matches two weeks ago with cash and had left behind a cigarette butt for authenticity. Besides, no one would investigate the burning of an old shed. They were probably happy it was gone. The thing had been a hazard, a heap of splinters and tetanus at the edge of Smith's land.

"Bye, Mister Greene! See you tomorrow!" students called. Keller smiled. The shed was a small feat compared to what he was planning next.

For seven months now, Keller had planned to burn the old Silverton house, a decaying two-story Victorian he'd discovered soon after moving to town. He first saw it while driving around to investigate possible targets. He liked weary, abandoned places where time gathered softly like dust. Past the church, past the pond, past the old town library with its bricks and bay windows, he'd discovered a driveway leading into the woods. Keller parked at the entrance. His feet crunched on the gravel as loudly as a person breathing in an empty room.

He ignored the "No Trespassing" sign, a futile sentry at the foot of the weed-grown yard. He inspected the house. The light blue paint was peeling, and one of the upper windows had been cracked, fractures spidering out from the central eye. The railing of the front porch had broken loose from the siding; it dangled over a patch of wild daisies as though it might jump to join them.

The town's decay disquieted most people. They dreaded shuttered stores and surrendered houses. They turned their eyes from boarded windows, rusted cars, sidewalks claimed by tree roots. Most of all, they feared the silence. It crept up on them in their homes, stealing silently like water pooling across the floor.

Keller liked the silence; he saw anonymity behind stands of trees. He saw lonely houses, aching for release from the emptiness of their rooms. He strode through the weeds and over broken steps onto the porch of the Silverton house, resting his hand on the cracked, dry wood of the windowsill.

He had waited for more than half a year. It would be dangerous to start another fire too soon. Meanwhile, his fingers longed for matches. Keller loved their slender wooden stems and proud red tips. It amazed him how such modest little sticks stood ready to burst into flame. Sometimes, he sat in his backyard and struck an entire box one by one with as much pleasure as people who eat chocolate in the privacy of their bedrooms. But now he had waited enough.

At seven o' clock, Keller drove to the library and parked his car. He liked to leave it far from the scene and checked the parking lot for witnesses. Not a person in sight. The library rarely had visitors; the town could only afford to keep it open part time. Keller left his phone on the passenger seat. From the trunk, he took a backpack full of crumpled newspapers. He walked for ten minutes to the Silverton house.

The sun slipped down, leaving a cold pink glow in its wake, and pine trees creaked as he walked up the driveway. Keller paused at the weed-grown yard and watched. The house was a blot of darkness against the fading day, the windows blank like guarded faces. He imagined the house bright; the tips of his fingers anticipated warmth. He would try the front door first.

Keller nearly reached the steps when he saw something move, a splotch of shadow blacker than the rest of the darkness. He froze, his heart loud in his ears.

"Hello?" His voice sounded louder than he had intended. "Hello?"

He thought he could make out a person, but no one responded.

"Who's there?" he demanded.

"I was just about to get going," a woman's voice said. "Don't mind me." She stood up and skipped down the steps. But then she glanced at him and stopped.

"Keller?" the woman asked. "Is that you?"

Keller pictured running away. He could deny it all. He could still pretend he'd never been at the Silverton house that day. But now he realized who the woman was. "Lara?"

The art teacher—the young woman who, at the last staff meeting, had asked everyone to donate scraps from their three-hole punches for some kind of "installation." The teachers exchanged glances. She was already disliked for protesting the principal's decision to replace the rotting ceiling tiles that leaked whenever it rained. He shouldn't do this, Lara said, because the mildewed scent would teach the students to think of passing time. Keller had seen her at meetings and in hallways, but he had never spoken to her before.

"What are you doing here?" he asked.

"I was—" She looked away and paused. "It's kind of weird, but I just love old houses. I was sitting on the porch, thinking."

"I like old houses, too." He tried to keep the irritation out of his voice, not wanting to arouse suspicion.

"Especially this one. It's gorgeous. When I see it, I can practically hear time passing."

"I know what you mean."

"You know," she said, "I've been trying to work up the courage to break in. Not to do anything—just to look around. I come here almost every day, but I haven't done it yet."

He stared at her. She wore a fitted wool coat in a dark shade of purple, her dark hair loosely hanging around her shoulders. If she came that often, how would he ever plant his supplies?

"Let's do it," Keller said, stepping onto the porch. "Let's break in."

"I'm surprised to see you here," Lara said, as he tried the front door, discovering it locked. Keller stepped to the side and pressed his palms against the grimy porch window. It slid grudgingly open. "In school you seem so—normal."

"I do?" Keller asked, laughing. He stepped over the sill and climbed inside, his backpack still on his shoulder. He held out both hands to help her through. Inside, fragments of light struggled through the far windows. For a moment, both of them stared at the shadows. Keller, realizing he still held Lara's hands, let go like she'd burned him. Lara smiled and turned to walk around the room. Dust stirred in the wake of her footsteps, swirling in soft, silent eddies. She traced a finger along the wall, leaving a narrow trail. Only a few artifacts remained: an overstuffed couch, a shabby wicker chair. She stepped carefully around the perimeter of a faded red rug with yellow tassels.

"I love this rug." She wandered into the next room. "Did you hear about the widow?" she called back. "The one who died here?"

"Yes," Keller said, following her. "I read how they found the body three weeks later."

"She must've had a lot of time to think before she died. I wonder what's upstairs?" The wooden floor creaked under her feet. They came onto a small landing and went into the first bedroom. An old, gray smoke detector occupied the center of the ceiling, the batteries probably dead. Curtains hung by the window, and Keller went over to investigate, finding them dry, almost brittle.

"This is gorgeous," Lara said, stroking the wall in the opposite corner of the room. "It'd be perfect for my installation." Keller turned to look. The pale, faded gold wallpaper reflected the dim light in flashes. It had a pattern of red roses tucked into curls of leaves.

"It is pretty nice." He would never have noticed if she hadn't pointed it out.

"We have to come back," she said.

"What do you mean?"

"For the wallpaper. To peel it off. Will you come back tomorrow, to help me? It's such hard work. But I definitely need it for my installation." She stood close to him now. Beneath her floral perfume, he detected an undertone of clay: an art teacher smell.

Keller felt helpless. "Of course I will."

The next morning, he found a note in his office mailbox:

Meet me in my classroom at 5. I want to show you my project. — Lara.

It was written in flowing cursive across a piece of faded yellow paper, the kind schools had when Keller was a boy. It smelled like it had been in a closet for several years. Anyone else would've emailed.

Intrigued, he went to her classroom at five. Pollock-style splatter murals in red, orange, and blue marked the hallway outside the art room. Inside, paint and paper shreds speckled the floor. Papier-mâché bowls covered several tables; autumn leaves cut from construction paper hung from the ceiling. Lara appeared to favor the burnable arts.

"Here I am!" she said from behind him, carrying a box of paint bottles, her hair wrapped into a wispy bun. She unbuttoned the black, long-sleeved shirt splattered with paint and threw it on the counter, revealing a violet V-neck sweater.

"Want to see my installation? It's at the library. I can drive us to the house after."

"Why don't we both drive, so you don't have to bring me back? We can walk to the house from there."

His backpack containing three soda bottles filled with paint thinner sat in the trunk. Keller wasn't about to let her disrupt his supply-planting, but he'd decided that participating in her project might be useful. She would believe he was a preservationist, someone who'd never burn an old house down.

At the library, an old brick cottage sat in the park. As Lara led him around back, he was surprised to see its facade scrubbed clean with new bushes planted in front. The warped glass windows had been polished. No longer opaque like cataract eyes, they had become clear and reflective.

"Did you know the Silvertons owned the library?" Lara asked. "The cottage was the caretaker's place."

"I remember reading something about it."

"It was abandoned for years. But I got a grant to make it into an exhibit."

Lara took a key from her pocket and opened the door, leading them into a single square room, furnished with a desk, a gilded mirror, and glass-doored bookcases. Lace curtains framed the windows. From the ceiling dangled strings of various lengths, holding keys, origami birds, and black-and-white photographs in plastic frames. The strings turned slowly, the keys and frames catching the light.

"It's a room where old things are safe," Lara said. "I found all of it around town. I really hope that wallpaper's dry-strippable. I want to paste it on these walls."

Brick buildings didn't burn, but things inside them did: desks, curtains—hole punches. A handful sat on the bedside table, scattered slightly.

"Is this what you need the hole punches for?" Keller asked.

"Yes. They're dust. I want to scatter them all over. In the summer, we'll open the windows so the wind will stir them around. The problem is, I can't make them myself. It has to be a community project. It's about how time affects all of us. But people aren't donating any. It might take a while to collect enough." She frowned, and Keller realized what was so beautiful about her face. Hidden behind her mouth, and reflected in her eyes, was a line of causeless sadness.

Back at the cars, Keller checked his watch: 5:30. They'd have an hour before sunset. He took the backpack from the trunk. "Supplies," he said. "I think we'll have enough sun, but I brought a flashlight, just in case." A whole backpack for a flashlight: brilliant excuse. His voice sounded loud and false; surely Lara could tell.

"I brought putty knives," Lara said unfazed, taking a cardboard box from her trunk.

They went down Silverton Road. The wind rustled in the pines as they went up the long gravel driveway. For first time, Keller's footsteps didn't sound so unbearably loud, now joined by Lara's. The porch window was closed, just as they had left it last time. Keller raised the window and held her hands to help her climb inside. Lara lingered near him, then continued into the living room. He shifted the backpack on his shoulder and wondered when he would hide his paint thinner.

Keller followed her as she floated toward the stairs, her footsteps creaking on the warped wooden floors. In the pale darkness, Lara looked unreal. How could he be sure she wasn't just a lovely ghost, that she wouldn't pass through a wall and vanish? The stairs spiraled into the dark; Lara faded as she climbed further up. She turned a corner and disappeared. Keller leapt up the stairs after her, plunged into the darkness of the hallway and found the door. Lara stood in the bedroom, smiling and stroking the wallpaper.

"I love paper," she said. "I just love how it kind of disintegrates when it's old. It's so delicate, it could burn up in an instant. That's what makes it beautiful."

Lara bent closer to the wall. "This has amazing texture. It reminds me of rice paper."

She wasn't paying attention to him. Seizing his chance, Keller darted out of the room. There had to be some place he could hide things. Usually, he stocked supplies over the course of several days. He liked to use various materials: paint thinner, nail polish remover, hairspray, newspaper. He relished taking time, stocking inconspicuously while planning how to unleash the conflagration.

Two other bedrooms occupied the second floor, each covered in wallpaper. He struck those out—Lara might go in to look at them. In one of the rooms lay a mattress. Keller crept downstairs, exploring the kitchen. The oven would do for now, he decided, and he stuffed the bottles of paint thinner inside and ran back upstairs.

"Everything okay?" Lara asked.

"I was looking for more wallpaper. There's some great blue stuff in the master bedroom."

"Maybe we can use that for other projects." She lifted a corner of the paper with her putty knife and pulled. Her eyes widened as it peeled away in a long strip.

"We're lucky!" she said. "We'll be able to dry-strip it. Careful—don't rip it too much!"

Keller tested the drywall beneath his hands, feeling the dry, brittle surface. The autumn air hung cool around them. Perfect burning conditions. He imagined a glorious, quick-spreading fire. Lara gently rolled her strip and put it in the box.

An hour later, as they walked back together with the box of wallpaper strips, Lara exulted. "I feel like a criminal!" she said. "It's kind of exciting!"

Keller made himself a promise then: he wouldn't burn the house until Lara had stripped all the wallpaper. It was a matter of prudence, he told himself. If he burned it too soon, she would be upset; she might ask questions. And he did want to see her finish the installation. The bare white walls were incomplete. Her room begged for golden finish with curling vines and red roses. The wallpaper was necessary for the wind, which otherwise would never stir the lace curtains and hole punch dust.

He worked with her on Mondays and Thursdays. The other days, he struggled to contain himself. Keller couldn't go to the house, otherwise he'd imagine smoke filling the rooms. His hands would sweat, anticipating the beautiful, dense heat. Then he would have to strike the first match. Against the image of red light, he held Lara's pale, thin smile. He'd waited this long; he could wait for another few weeks.

Late on Sundays, Keller hunted recycled newspapers shivering helplessly on the curb. He hated seeing words thrown away, stripped of their dignity and next to the trash and rescued the newspapers from homelessness. With reverence, he dismembered them and crumpled them up. He piled them in conical stacks six feet high, framed by dry branches. He lit matches to send the words off, releasing them with sympathy—the same way he freed abandoned houses from the emptiness of their rooms.

But backyard bonfires weren't enough. Fire consumed the paper greedily. After the initial joy of flame and smoke, it vanished within minutes. Keller needed more than anything to light a momentous fire, one that would burn grandly in an old Victorian house. But he also thought of Lara, who excited him almost as much as burning. He imagined peeling wallpaper with this peculiar woman in pale darkness as she spoke in her low voice about the widow.

"I think it's beautiful how she died," Lara said.

"Really? Why?"

"It was a natural process of decay, like leaves falling from a tree. She just happened to be the last one left."

"But don't you think she was lonely?"

"She had memories. Sometimes, the silence at the end of things is the best part."

"That's an interesting take on it."

The sunlight faded, and Lara looked out the window. "Time goes so quickly. When I was a kid, sometimes I'd turn around fast to try and catch a glimpse of the past me."

"It's true," Keller said. "You can almost see time evaporating before your eyes."

"But that's why everything matters so much."

They stood close together. As he reached to grab a corner of paper, Keller touched her hand. She didn't move away.

"My hands are so dry. It's the clay."

He took her hand and rubbed his thumb over the back of it.

"I need to moisturize."

"No, you don't." Her fingers were perfect. The magenta polish on her nails had chipped, revealing gray slivers of clay underneath. Dry, but warm: art teacher hands.

One Thursday, after the students had gone home, Lara appeared in the door of Keller's classroom. He had been sitting at his desk thinking of her. He imagined her molding clay, glazing it, and putting it in the kiln. It would bake under hot flames, and when she took it out later, the glazes shone red and yellow.

"I can't make it tonight," she said. "I'm behind on a grant proposal. It's awful, but I have to finish. I'd rather spend the evening with you." She frowned and walked along the wall, tracing the gaps between the concrete blocks with her fingers.

"Maybe another time?" He watched her walk the perimeter. Thinking of not seeing her, a chill of disappointment settled on his skin like cold ash.

"What about tomorrow?" she said. "Meet me at the library?"

"Yes," he said, too quickly.

"I have a project to show you at my house. Maybe you can come over after?"

"Sure. I'm around."

"See you tomorrow, then." Lara approached his desk and brushed the front edge with her hand, smiling at him. She let the white tips of her fingers linger on the frame before she disappeared.

Beneath Keller's eagerness, his stomach churned faintly with unease. Before Lara, there had been Jane, a sweet-voiced redhead who noticed Keller's details gradually, until the day she understood them all at once.

"Wow, need any more matches?" she'd asked, finding sixteen boxes in the pantry.

"I buy them in bulk. Otherwise, it's impossible to remember."

She wondered why he had nail polish remover in the bathroom, why he burned the brush in his backyard so frequently. She'd spotted all the clues, but in the absence of their sum, it would've taken a person like Keller to piece them together. And in Easton, the suburban town where he taught for four years, there was not a single person like him. A friend had introduced him to Jane, whose sweetness and pale beauty felt to Keller like rewards for feigning sanity. He wrapped his fingers in her curls and stroked her smooth legs and pretended he was happy.

But the old emptiness crept up inside him. As much as he kissed Jane and gazed into her cheerful blue eyes, he couldn't help it. He bought three more boxes of matches at the grocery store and hair spray at the pharmacy. After the farmer who lived at the edge of town died, Keller told Jane he couldn't see her that weekend; he had tests to grade.

The old barn seemed stricken with dementia, loose

shingles and rotting wood signaling its demise. It had to be released. He readied his supplies, and late one night, he lit another match.

He was strolling away when Jane saw him in the street. He knew she walked alone, but he didn't know she did it at night.

"Keller!" Jane called. "The one time I forget my phone, there's an emergency."

"Yeah, I was just about to call 911," he said.

"You didn't already?" She looked at him oddly. "You smell like smoke."

Keller made the call and said he was going home.

"Don't you want to see them put it out?"

"Not really."

She stared at him. "You did this," she said, realization changing her face. "You did, didn't you? It all adds up. You've lost your mind. Go, Keller, before I call the police."

———❧———

In the two months he searched for a new job elsewhere, Keller kept waiting for the police to arrive at his door, but they never did. Jane had liked him at least that much.

He lay awake at night, feeling like there was no ceiling above him—only an empty universe, space lurking and waiting to vacuum him up. The revelation of his truest self had frightened her away.

But Lara was different. Maybe they'd do another art project together, and he would try to tell her. Alone, he tested the words: "I like to burn things." He would explain it slowly, starting with the small fires years ago. Eventually, if he did it right, she might understand.

While Keller waited at the library for Lara to arrive, he scanned the news on his phone and regretted it immediately. He didn't need to know about natural disasters and violent crimes. He was about to switch to email when something caught his eye. A local woman died in a car accident. He read the article. She'd been thrown from the car after hitting a tree. He swore when he saw the name. Jane.

Keller still thought of her occasionally. They had gone to contradances together, and he used to love how her orange and blue paisley dresses flared generously from her waist. He imagined her flying through the windshield, the glass slicing her skin, her lacerated body crumpled on the ground.

He leaned against the trunk of his car, curled his hands into fists, and crossed his arms, hugging himself. With restless anxiety, Keller checked the time. 7:15pm, their meeting time plus fifteen minutes for Lara's customary lateness. But she had not arrived, nor were there any texts from her. Keller felt like a sink hole had opened up in of his stomach. He needed to see her. Now.

Keller walked around the library and peered in the windows. Rows of books huddled in the gloom. They looked dry and lonely, unused. He went around back to the cottage. The setting sun cast a glare on the brashly opaque windows. He cupped his hands to look in. He thought something moved inside and jumped, but it was only the lace curtains.

He checked again: 8:00. He sent Lara a text, but she didn't respond. Fifteen minutes later, he called her. She didn't answer. He took a few deep breaths and paced back and forth next to his car, leaning against it when dizziness overcame him. Lara might've gotten in an accident, too. It was possible that she was dead.

It was a dry day in October. The trees had turned orange, the color of Jane's hair. He liked to think of turning trees as slow fires, shifting from green to orange to black. The scenes of his incendiary passion blazed before him. In high school, he'd done the neighbor's doghouse after the gentle golden retriever died. In college, there'd been a sad, squat ranch in Vermont. This was the way to relieve his emptiness. Keller's hands grew damp. He could do it now.

He got in his car and drove to the Silverton house. He parked recklessly halfway up the driveway. Lara was wrong about the widow. There was no beauty in her death, only sadness. Her husband had died pointlessly eleven years before her, shot by a burglar at the florist's. Her spendthrift son had been lost in a plane accident. She'd locked herself inside and withered alone in the dust-strewn light.

Keller, too, would die alone. He thought of Lara in her purple coat, smiling in the dust. He had been a fool. Love and arson were incompatible truths—since the latter was indispensable, the former was out. His feet crunched anxiously on the gravel, and for once, the mournful pines stood still. The Silverton house leaked dark loneliness from the windows. It was up to him to rescue it from time.

There were matches and bottles of paint thinner in the oven, newspapers in all the kitchen cabinets. In a closet on the first floor, he'd hidden hairspray and nail polish remover, a paintbrush and large plastic bags. Wearing leather gloves, Keller snatched his supplies from hiding. He ran through the house, opening all the doors and windows, taking the bottles of paint thinner upstairs. The door to the wallpaper room was already open. As he passed it, he paused. He knew what the room looked like: three walls bare, a single stretch of gold left next to the windows—next to the brittle, burnable curtains.

Though he hadn't lit the fire yet, he could imagine the rousing scent of smoke. Premonitions of flames leapt before his eyes. He didn't open the windows of the wallpaper room, striding to the far bedroom instead.

Keller dragged the mattress into the hallway, propping it against the wall near the top of the stairs. He unscrewed the cap from one bottle of paint thinner and poured it over the mattress. As it dripped down the side, the pungent scent filled his nostrils. His hands trembled as he unscrewed the other caps and balanced the open bottles on the mattress. He ran downstairs for the newspapers and hairspray, bringing them back to the second floor. Grinning, he scattered the newspapers down the stairs, spritzing them with hairspray as he descended to the first floor.

At the bottom of the staircase, he used the paintbrush to dab some nail polish remover on an electrical outlet, arranging a few pieces of newspaper between it and the stairs to create a trail. His hands were sweating now, his heart thumping like a little boy's on Christmas morning. Dabbing more nail polish remover on his paintbrush, he swept the perimeter of the room to connect the electrical outlets—always a useful trick for confusing investigators. Next, he shoved the couch to sit by the wood-paneled wall that sheltered the stairs, stacking the wicker chair on top of it. He emptied the nail polish remover over them, stuffing more newspapers in the spaces between. Finally, he rolled up the red rug and propped it against the entire starter pile.

Keller struck the first match. It flared up between his fingers, and he held it carefully to the newspapers under the chair. They lit, and Keller stepped back. Flames engulfed the couch, and the wicker chair burned like it was in love. Smoke rolled; Keller laughed. It was his best fire yet.

He took out a handful of matches, scraped them all against the box, and tossed them. They scattered happily, one landing near the stairs. The electric outlet burst into flame, and soon, the newspapers caught. The fire traveled toward the stairs. There would be an explosion, exactly as he had laid the path. Keller's heart beat proudly. The house was full of light, no longer the dark abode of dust. It was all because of him.

The black smoke grew dense—time to make his exit. Keller burst from the house and dashed down the porch steps. Halfway through the yard, he turned to look. The fire spread quickly. Light leapt into the second floor. Soon the windows would explode in flashover, and all the evidence would be destroyed. Keller laughed happily.

The fire wasn't just outside him; it was inside him, too. He felt warm and buoyant. He ran from the house.

Lara stood at the opening of the driveway, her hands shoved deep in the pockets of her purple coat. By the glow of the blaze, she looked small and dim. The firelight shone in the tears on her cheeks. Her eyes were as blank as empty windows. Suddenly, Keller felt like he'd been dunked in icy water.

"Keller," Lara said. "Did you do this?"

"Oh, so now you show up."

"What are you talking about? I texted you, from my friend's phone."

"When?"

"About half an hour ago. I was working in my office and one of the pipes broke in the art room. Everything flooded. I had to save the art projects. It never occurred to you I might not be able to answer?"

Keller shook his head.

"What the hell are you doing?"

He noticed she was backing away slowly. His voice went quiet. "Well, I—"

"What are you, crazy? I thought you loved this house, like I did." Lara's voice shook. She squinted, like it hurt her to look at him.

He couldn't bear to wait for the rest of her denunciation. In a blaze of fear, Keller ran.

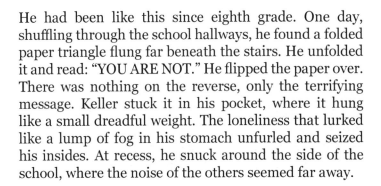

He had been like this since eighth grade. One day, shuffling through the school hallways, he found a folded paper triangle flung far beneath the stairs. He unfolded it and read: "YOU ARE NOT." He flipped the paper over. There was nothing on the reverse, only the terrifying message. Keller stuck it in his pocket, where it hung like a small dreadful weight. The loneliness that lurked like a lump of fog in his stomach unfurled and seized his insides. At recess, he snuck around the side of the school, where the noise of the others seemed far away.

There, like an answer, lay the match on the sidewalk. It was placed in the center, parallel to the trough in the concrete. He picked it up. The tip was red, a sign of what it wanted to be. He took the message out of his pocket, struck the match against the ground, and held the paper to it. It lit slowly, edges curling and blackening. The heat nipped his fingers and he dropped it, where it fell flaring at his feet. It didn't matter how his heart stung with sadness. Against it, he held fire as his talisman: heat, light, and joy.

This was his unchangeable self. But still, he thought incurably of Lara: how she moved in the gloom of the vanished Silverton house, how she loved colors and wore that purple coat, how she fancied paper and the past. Why was it that things became more beautiful after they were lost? As Keller thought of Lara, tears burned his cheeks, and his soul felt like ashes.

"Punch!" Keller shouted. "Punch like it's your last minute to live!"

The room was strewn with colors: red, purple, orange, green, blue. One girl had a stack of yellow all to herself, slamming several sheets at once with vigor. A cardboard W.B. Mason box sat on Keller's desk. The bottom was already covered with multicolored hole punches, and each second, students threw in handfuls more.

"Why are we doing this?" someone asked.

"For Miss Tyler," Keller said. "For her installation."

At the end of the class, the box still wasn't full. He shook it, staring into the shifting hole punches. He'd imagined heaping piles of them, but they barely filled an eighth of the volume.

The hours dragged their feet. At five o' clock, he went to see her. His hands were damp as he carried the box to her classroom. He tried not to hurry, but his feet disobeyed.

"Keller," Lara said, spotting him as soon as he crossed the door frame.

"Lara," he said, staring into the box. "My class made these for you."

"Thanks." Her face was still. He could not read how she felt.

"Lara, do you hate me?"

"Because of what you did? Honestly—yeah."

"I wanted to tell you. I thought you'd understand. I'm not a criminal. I only do abandoned houses."

"But those are the best kind," she said softly, looking into the box. "The ones you shouldn't burn. Keller, I have work to do. You should go."

Keller looked at her feet. She wore brown Oxford shoes, small and delicate like the rest of her. He'd often wondered what her feet were like—if they were as perfect and warm as her hands. But now he would never know.

Keller stood alone in his backyard, holding a matchbox in his hand. After Lara, he thought things would be the way they were before. But now silence grew loud in the empty rooms of his house; unaccompanied evenings hung heavy on his shoulders. He felt as though the daylight weren't bright enough—everything was dim, matches only brief flickers giving respite to his darkness.

His house reminded him of the widow's. The paint on the siding was chipped, revealing the dry wood underneath. The windows had the same blank look, like the person inside was dead. He opened the matchbox and selected one: a wisp of wood in his fingers, a red tip like a flower. He struck it and held it up, so the flame was superimposed over the window of his bedroom. He liked how it looked there.

A car came up his driveway, startling him. He dropped the match. For a moment, he wondered if it was Lara. But instead, it was a police car. Two officers got out.

"Keller Greene?" one of the them asked. He nodded.

As they drove him away, he thought of her. Maybe she was putting up the wallpaper right this moment, unrolling it carefully, adjusting each piece so the patterns would line up. In the cottage, the light would glint on the gold; it would reflect on her hair and her face. It had been several days since he'd seen her, and already the details had begun to fade—the exact position of the mole on her cheek, the particular shade of paleness of her skin. Even though she had betrayed him, he wished he could remember.

UNHANDING

J ack waited for a few minutes after he heard Carolynn tramp outside to feel sure he was safe. Each day, his wife packed a cooler with unsweetened iced tea and cucumber sandwiches; she then slung a beach chair over her shoulder and dawdled a half-mile along sandy streets to the rickety wooden steps ascending the dunes. Once silence filled the cottage, Jack could investigate the strange feeling that overtook him: the sensation that the hand attached to his left arm was not his own.

Nothing obvious marked the hand as an imposter. The skin was the correct shade of slightly tan, and the nails, with their familiar rough texture, were trimmed square as he liked, but he wasn't certain that the fingers would move at the command of his brain. When they curled as he told them to, it felt like more of a coincidence than cause and effect.

While Jack answered emails on his laptop, he noticed the left hand kept up with the right as it tapped across the keys. It didn't lack any sort of flexibility or reach. Reason identified this hand as his—but the sensation in the fingertips felt dull, like the skin had been covered by a thin film or a glove.

The screen door slammed, and Carolynn stuck her head in the living room. Jack started.

"Something wrong?"

Jack shook his head. Her uncanny therapist's knack for sensing when something was amiss still surprised him, though they'd been together for a year. "That was quick."

Carolynn laughed. "Forgot sunscreen. You should put away the laptop and take a break for once."

"Maybe." Jack hated the beach. He hated the grit of sand in his toes, which somehow always migrated into his eyes and pubic hair. He hated sunscreen choking his skin and the salt on his tongue even though he didn't swim.

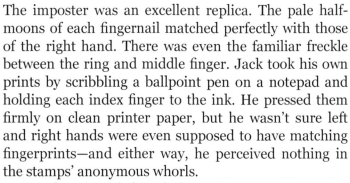

The imposter was an excellent replica. The pale half-moons of each fingernail matched perfectly with those of the right hand. There was even the familiar freckle between the ring and middle finger. Jack took his own prints by scribbling a ballpoint pen on a notepad and holding each index finger to the ink. He pressed them firmly on clean printer paper, but he wasn't sure left and right hands were even supposed to have matching fingerprints—and either way, he perceived nothing in the stamps' anonymous whorls.

He determined his feeling of ownership ended precisely at the wrist.

At dinner, Carolynn prattled on about the strangers she watched. She cataloged marital tensions, oedipal complexes, and the red flags of adultery like an avid naturalist spotting birds. Every now and then, she cast a meaningful glance at Jack, inviting him to disclose the source of the discontent she observed, but he was determined not to tell her. He grilled the steak and sautéed the kale; wasn't that enough? If he told her, she would name his condition—every state not perfectly normal had a name—and in doing so, trivialize it.

It was what she always did. She had used her DSM-5 to diagnose his occasional morose moods as minor depression with melancholic features. He hated that silly name. It had nothing to do with how, when he caught the scent of fall in the summer air, it made him restless, or how a combination of fading light and faraway sounds borne on the wind could make him feel tired and discontented. She even had the audacity to say this wasn't the "real him," but an "illness," that he should get counseling or take medication to make it go away. Jack didn't like her deciding what was and wasn't him. He could decide that for himself, and even if part of him was diseased, he could choose to keep it.

That night, lying awake, Jack's worst thought yet struck him: if this hand wasn't real, where was his real one? He tried to go back to sleep but couldn't shake the image of his real hand lying somewhere, neglected, detached.

He slipped out of bed, putting his feet on the floor. Carolynn mumbled something in her sleep, but didn't stir.

The hand had to be somewhere in the cottage; that was when he noticed it missing. Jack looked under the throw pillows on the couch. He looked in the kitchen cupboards and even in the oven. He rushed from room to room, pounding the light switches on. All the lights in the house blazed, as bright as the loss that seared his heart.

He tugged the futon away from the wall. Its wooden leg gouged the hardwood floor.

Carolynn appeared at the door, nagging him like an aggrieved parent. "What is it, Jack? What's wrong?" she said, one hand over her breast.

Jack crouched close to the floor. It occurred to him that this might not be the real Carolynn. "Who are you?" he whispered.

"Jack?"

"Who are you?" he said out loud. He said it again and again, not certain the voice ringing in his ears was his own.

AN INQUIRY INTO
THE NATURE OF
HAPPINESS

Deep in the stacks, sitting in an empty carrel that wasn't hers, Eleanor spotted a golden ring. It lay in the corner under the desktop shelf, nearly obscured by shadow. She picked it up and held it close to the window. Ivy crept over the narrow panes, but even in the hindered light, the ring shone in her hand.

An inscription inside read: Julia D. Minkoff, an unfamiliar name. The outer engravings showed Julia was also a senior; she lived in the dormitory next door. Eleanor sometimes ate in their wood-paneled dining hall, so her own housemates wouldn't notice how often she sat alone.

She pocketed the ring and turned back to reading about the conquests of the Mongols. She found stories of brides kidnapped, heads severed, and villagers executed strangely comforting, proof that the current epoch was not alone in its brutality. Maybe Julia also read such accounts. Maybe when that exhausted her, she also sank to the floor against a shelf, selected a random book and opened it, smelled the paper and looked at all the words—imagining millions of words in this library alone, until the dispirited collection in her own head felt reassuringly insignificant.

When Eleanor exited the stacks, she considered giving the ring to the attendant at the desk. But the weight in her pocket was too pleasant, a secret, knowing she had something belonging to someone else, something no one else could see.

Julia's Facebook pictures showed a girl with sleek brown hair and subtle makeup, smiling as she leaned against the side of the brick pedestrian bridge. The river extended behind her in a blue swath to the horizon. She held a book to her chest. Eleanor had guessed right; Julia did like books. Her profile said she studied English, a subject complementary to Eleanor's History. Eleanor might meet her for lunch in the dining hall and produce the ring to exclamations of gratitude. Maybe they would discover that they both loved minor-key symphonies, gothic novels, and sordid endings.

But other pictures showed Julia in a crimson dress, holding a bottle of vodka aloft among friends; Julia grinning over a fruit-covered waffle, knife and fork in fists; Julia and a sports team, wearing jerseys and face paint. Julia was rarely alone. She didn't play loud music on her phone to block out the sounds of others talking. She didn't walk alone by the river at night, throwing rocks to shatter its still, black surface. Julia appeared well-adjusted and busy. She enjoyed scenic landscapes, savory food, and parties with friends. Clicking through her pictures revealed a dauntless, months-long smile, lips that never wearied of peeling back from perfect, round, white teeth.

From her tower room, Eleanor stared out to the concrete nine floors below, wondering if they'd made the windows so narrow on purpose. She knew she should return the ring, but two weeks later, it still occupied a spot on her desk, right where the sun would hit it. She liked to sit and study it, admiring how it sat there, glittering.

Julia represented a certain mystery, one that troubled Eleanor even before she found the ring. How could someone, despite all evidence about the world, flit through life with such wholesome cheer? Upon news of the latest shooting, Eleanor's head felt leaden, and her heart pumped anxiety in hot spurts through her veins. She thought others, too, must feel this dreadful weight, but the dining hall brimmed full; its lights burned vibrant and yellow; students gathered and chatted, as though fifteen children's bodies had not been extricated from an elementary school bathroom that morning. Meanwhile, Eleanor found it difficult to complete her thesis on the history of Nanking. Her advisor had emailed again, demanding the next chapter. It seemed that the ring was a riddle, and Julia was its answer, the answer to why Eleanor couldn't live with the calm ease displayed by everyone else.

She didn't allow herself to call it stalking—merely people watching with a purpose, an inquiry into the methods of Julia's effervescence. On the first night, Eleanor set up in the dining hall before dinner, taking the table in the corner next to the grand piano. She purchased a plate of overcooked broccoli and chicken as soon as the kitchen doors opened. While she ate, she pretended to do homework to keep the friendly tutors away. Otherwise, they might come talking, hoping to bestow their presence upon an alienated soul.

Eventually, Julia sauntered in with a large pack of friends, all of them pink-cheeked and laughing. They settled around a nearby table and poked their forks at tiny piles of food. Eleanor felt like an anthropologist studying a tribe of natives, attempting to decode their customs. What made them so happy? Even if they were truly friends, soon they would graduate and disperse across the state to professions of varying banality.

Eleanor wanted to tell Dave about the ring, but she hadn't seen him in two weeks. He hadn't answered any of her texts. His strange silence had even prompted her to call his house, but no one picked up. Usually, they spent hours talking at dinner. She missed how he folded his hands behind his head as he heard her woes, his fitted blazer stretching back fashionably. She imagined telling him. *I found a class ring in the library. I know who it belongs to. She's in the house next door. But I haven't given it back.*

Dave would tilt his chair back and grin. He, too, found moral ambiguity more intriguing than doing the right thing. *Ooh, who is she?* he'd ask, the flamboyant timbre in his voice creeping to a higher pitch than usual.

Eleanor would tell him about watching Julia at dinner. She would tell him how she kept the ring in her pocket, feeling it was more important to her than to its owner.

Dave would sympathize. He had once been responsible for the disappearance of a rival oboist's best reed right before a concert. The oboist had committed the crime of telling him he was a downer; she'd like to see him smile more.

Happy bitch, he'd say about Julia. *Don't give it back.* She deserves to know what it's like to lose something.

Eleanor called Dave's cell, even though she didn't expect him to answer. This time, she couldn't even leave a message saying to call her back. His voicemail was full.

The group usually came to dinner at 6:15. Julia was its sun and center, and her companions revolved around her, their pastel blouses and chandelier earrings glittering in her reflected light. It seemed a coveted honor to sit by her side, to absorb the first tremors of her conversation, to cause the bright ripples of her laughter, but such enchanting appearances provided no answers. One day, Eleanor decided to follow them.

After Julia and her friends put their trays on the conveyor belt outside the kitchen, she trailed them out of the mahogany doors to the green. She followed them through the gate and down one of the residential side streets to the river. In the warm spring evening, their conversation and laughter floated before her like dandelion seeds in the wind. Eleanor felt for the hard lump in her pocket. She had taken to carrying the ring with her. Somehow, she believed it would tell her the answer, whisper the solution when the time was right. Julia was happy because she had many friends. These friends operated as a filter between Julia and the world. Whatever did not fit through the lattice of their smiles was kept from her as nonexistent.

The girls stopped by a row of magnolias on the riverbank. They took group pictures under pink-flowered boughs, locking arms and lifting iPhones. Several of them flocked on ahead, leaving Julia behind. She touched the bark of a tree and gazed toward the river, standing still. Maybe she was looking at the brick pedestrian bridge spanning the green banks or the daffodils and crocuses by the water's edge.

Julia probably thought the river was beautiful, but Eleanor saw it otherwise. She saw the haze from the highway running too close by; she saw grim skyscrapers marring the horizon and magnolia petals falling from clouds of pearly pink. Once they drifted to the ground, joggers trod them into shiny brown slicks.

After some time, Julia's friends noticed her absence and called her. Laughing, she turned and sprinted to join them.

Eleanor often wished she had met Dave in high school, so they could've indulged their psychoses together. No one else understood why she read awful things. Her mother called it strange and ungrateful. Eleanor grew up in a town with pastel houses and lush lawns, where children played in the streets on summer evenings, unafraid of the cars that always slowed for them. There was no reason she should believe goodness was an illusion on loan.

If Dave had been there, they could've gone to the library together. He would research the ways he expected civilization to end: nuclear war, famine, plague. He would laugh as he read choice excerpts out loud, saying, "Why, it's practically over, my dear."

Meanwhile, she would research arcane genres of horror: serial rapists, men who killed women for the purpose of eating their flesh, human medical experiments during the Holocaust. She would puzzle over the astonishing disparity between her own life, devoid of suffering, and the horror of reality elsewhere. At the time, she thought such knowledge would protect her. If she knew the worst that could happen, the absolute nadir of human experience, then nothing could ever harm her.

Once, when Eleanor was lucky, she caught the sight of Julia by herself.

When she approached her corner table that night, a girl already sat there, hunched over and wearing a hoodie. Eleanor circled around cautiously and almost dropped her tray. It was Julia, with not a friend in sight.

Julia devoured a salad, stabbing the lettuce leaves and tomatoes on her plate with uncharacteristic vehemence. When she finished, Eleanor stole after her as she left the dining hall and headed off campus, passing Victorian houses and a community vegetable garden. She lurked outside as Julia entered the narrow waffle shop at the V of two intersecting streets. After a few minutes, she went in and skimmed the menu, sneaking glances at the single long table by the window.

When Eleanor sat down with her plain waffle, she got a closer look. Julia ate a large waffle covered in whipped cream and blueberries. In between bites of dough, she scooped plain whipped cream onto her fork and licked it off, making Eleanor wish she had ordered the same thing. She touched the ring in her pocket. Julia was happy because, even on bad days, she could do certain things to make herself feel better, like eating waffles. These coping mechanisms proved specific and effective, alleviating any lapse from feelings of cheer. Julia slumped and rested her head in one hand while she ate. For a strange moment, the gesture almost reminded Eleanor of Dave.

This encounter thrilled her so much that Eleanor plotted to engineer a similar occurrence. She created a fake Gmail account and put Julia's address into the recipient box.

Hey Julia, she typed. This is Amy Walker. I'm in your class. Hope senior year's going okay. I found a class ring with your name in the library. Did you lose it? Maybe we can meet up so I can give it back. Let me know.

Eleanor nodded, pleased. For the first time in months, she had recovered a feeling of agency. This single situation was under her power: she would decide what happened to the ring.

Later that evening, Eleanor got an email from Dave.

Hey Ellie. Sorry I've gone AWOL. Truth is, I'm not actually at school right now. I withdrew from this semester after a lovely stint in the hospital. Not to worry, all is being healed in the happy house where they stowed me. The food is as gourmet as that of our dining hall. Plus, they have these gorgeous wooden bars blocking the sides of the stairwells, so you can't pull a fast one and jump. There are so many crazy people here I NEED to tell you about. Let's talk sometime?

Eleanor stared down at her desk. Last fall, visiting home unexpectedly, Dave had walked in on his father to see him with a gun at his feet, life not successfully taken. The coma was approaching eight months now. She tried so hard to watch Dave for this. She wished she could protect him: Dave with his pale hands moisturized to perfection, obsessing about reeds; Dave taking her to the symphonies with the best oboe solos and quietly weeping throughout, while Eleanor pretended for his pride not to notice; Dave calling her Ellie, a nickname only he was allowed to use.

Just then, another email arrived in her inbox. It was a reply from Julia.

Hey Amy! Thanks so much for your email! I've been looking for that ring everywhere!!! Want to grab a snack at the waffle place? It's my favorite!! How about 3:00?

Eleanor snorted at all the exclamation points. She couldn't understand this infuriating veneer of cheerfulness.

She had counted on graduating with Dave. Who else would stand beside her in the black-robed procession? Who else would whisper sarcastic replies to blandly optimistic speeches? She imagined him alone in a dark room, contemplating ways to die. She, of all people, would've sat with him through the night, if only he had told her.

When he didn't answer his phone, she sent an email. He replied within the hour. He had answered none of her questions. Instead, he had a single comment about Eleanor's updates. Maybe you should give that ring back. A cold feeling spread like a sheet of black ink across her body. Even her friend had sided with the irresistible Julia.

Before the meeting, Eleanor arrived at the waffle shop early and ordered a large waffle with blueberries and whipped cream. She sat at the table, stabbed her fork down, and took a bite. Sweetness filled her mouth: fresh cream, sweet dough, the gush of juice as she pierced blueberries between her teeth. But sugar couldn't mitigate Dave's unexpected rebuke. His message harried her like a persistent, invisible splinter.

The bell above the door tinkled as someone entered: Julia, who glanced over at her. Eleanor looked down and studied her book to ward off inquiry.

Julia ordered a small strawberry-banana waffle and brought her plate to the opposite corner of the table, staring out the window while eating slowly. She wore a blazer and mint green skinny jeans. Of course she would wear the most fashionable color of that spring. Julia was happy because she dressed like a magazine model. This created a favorable impression on others, leading to social approval and its associated benefits: a positive feedback loop of good results. Eleanor reached inside the pocket of her windbreaker and touched the cool, smooth metal. She wished Dave could know she still had it, that she had not followed his disloyal suggestion.

Julia sighed and checked her phone. She got up and walked toward Eleanor, who almost choked on the bite she had just taken. She wondered if she had somehow been discovered. Julia might accuse her of keeping the ring, which Eleanor held in her pocketed hand at that very moment. But let her make accusations. Eleanor would never give it back.

"Excuse me," Julia said. "Are you Amy? I'm supposed to meet someone."

Eleanor fidgeted with the ring in her pocket. For all her effortful dislike, there was something ineffably attractive about Julia. Before Dave's email, she might've wanted to say yes, to give it back, to become Julia's newest friend.

But bitterness rose like bile in her throat. Dave, her best friend, had rejected her. Her own mother had said her presence was as dismal as November rain, a negative drizzle that could depress a healthy soul. She would keep the ring to spite them all.

"No," Eleanor said. "No, I'm not."

A few days before graduation, while Eleanor sat in her laundry-strewn dorm room, her mother called. She wanted to know whether Eleanor planned on attending the senior picnic. Eleanor said no. She didn't want to see Julia and her friends in floral sundresses. She would hate the crimson lunchboxes packed with ham sandwiches and cookies, the dessert trays with chocolate éclairs and cheesecakes. She wouldn't miss hearing some politician read platitudes from an index card.

Her mother, sensing negativity, proposed counseling. Eleanor might try again with Suzanne, the pink-clad therapist she might not dislike so much, if she would only give her a chance.

Eleanor didn't see why chances should be given. Suzanne wore sneakers with skirts. Her hair looked like an animal pelt. She advised Eleanor to exercise more and recommended the pleasures of golf. That, plus a little positive thinking, could make all the difference.

———✦———

That night, Eleanor received an email from the school: "Sad News," the subject that always prefaced an announcement of death. A few months ago, a junior who'd been struck and dragged under a pick-up truck for a mile had had a "tragic accident." Now it was a member of the class of 2012, Eleanor's class, who had "died suddenly." She felt so unsettled by the evasive phrase, she read it twice before registering the name: Julia D. Minkoff.

The school paper had already published an obituary and a tribute, an officially sanctioned collection of pictures and quotes from friends. It was all the more devastating, they said, because she had been a local girl, had grown up a few blocks away and fulfilled the family tradition by going to the college down the street.

The quotes were predictable, and Eleanor had seen all the pictures before, the ones she used to resent most: smiles in broad sunshine, palm trees and mountaintops in the background. A few days later, when the real story came out—bloated white body found in the river, no foul play suspected—Eleanor clicked through the pictures again and again, feeling like she'd swallowed a smooth, heavy stone. She searched the images for clues she should've spotted, the same clues she'd failed to see in Dave. Everywhere, she saw Julia's guarded eyes, eyes camouflaged by the flashing of teeth. After this, Eleanor realized, it looked like a different kind of smile now.

She felt the ring in her pocket as she crept down the crooked brick sidewalk the next day. Eleanor couldn't stop thinking about the waffle house. She imagined a thousand times saying yes that day. She dreaded to think the ring had been the subject of one of Julia's final hopes. She could do only one thing now: slip it into the casket when no one else was looking.

The setting sun glinted on the little stone church next to the funeral home. In the parlor, the shades had been drawn; the air was thick with the scent of peonies; the casket glistened like a wet stone. A line of weeping girls wound around the room. Eleanor recognized some of Julia's friends. She stood in the back of the line. As it edged forward, Eleanor realized she had never been to a wake before, and she didn't know what to do. She always thought they left the casket open so you could see the person inside.

Two women stood to the side. One looked about the same age as Eleanor's mother. "Thank you for coming," she said, holding out a hand. Eleanor didn't take it.

"Why is it closed?"

The woman looked at her. "Excuse me?"

"I asked why it's closed." Eleanor's voice sounded so loud in the quiet room, much louder than anything else. The ring felt like a millstone in her pocket. There was no place where she could put it.

The woman snapped her mouth shut and walked away. The older woman whispered, "Sweetie, the body..." But then she stopped.

"But I want to see her," Eleanor said.

"It's okay, honey, I do, too." The old woman grabbed one of Eleanor's hands and held it between her own.

Eleanor wrenched it away and turned around. All the people stared at her, ruining it. They didn't understand.

She had counted on this. She had wanted to return the ring.

And, she realized, she had wanted to see the body, to witness its truth. She had read about people found in the water. The human face, drowned, could swell to nearly the size of an elementary school desk.

She rushed for the door of the room, stumbling against a chair on her way out. What right did they have to ignore the result of Julia's suffering? How could they turn away from what she had wrought? She thought of Julia's battered, hidden face—the face these fearful people had chosen not to see. Only a person like her could bear to look and comprehend.

And yet outside, under the fading, pale pink sky, she couldn't imagine sinking into the cold dark river, looking through the watery veil to the shining world above. What unconquerable despair must Julia have felt to relinquish the light and air? It occurred to Eleanor that, for all her own supposed suffering, she couldn't have done it. She loved the small things too much: library books no one else had borrowed; rocks that disrupted the river when she tossed them in at night; even the delicate sparrows, who flitted and chirped at the edge of a nearby puddle, splashing droplets over their wings.

Eleanor could never understand Julia's fathomless anguish. For all her studied sorrow, she was a fraud.

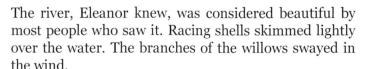

The river, Eleanor knew, was considered beautiful by most people who saw it. Racing shells skimmed lightly over the water. The branches of the willows swayed in the wind.

Eleanor saw other things: a plastic bag ensnared on a stick; yellow construction tape blocking off part of the bridge. But it was true that the banks were mostly green, and sunlight cast bright patches across the river's trembling surface.

A more perfect person would've contacted the family, would've invented some reason, if not the truth, that Eleanor had the ring. But Eleanor wasn't not perfect, perhaps wasn't even decent or reasonable. She believed she was meant to have it, to possess this thing so heavy it crushed each grain of her own small fears, a symbol of despair so great, she could never approach it. It was a relic of Julia, whose cheerful face had been an artificial construction, a mask of hair and paint and teeth.

What did she know of that stranger, whose sadness so far outstripped her own? Almost nothing, except this: She had stood alone by this river, under these magnolias. She had smiled to hide the wounds festering under her skin. She had worn this golden talisman so smooth and heavy—this ring that Eleanor now, for the first time, slipped onto her unadorned finger.

Emily Eckart is from Massachusetts. Her writing has appeared in The Washington Post, Nature, Potomac Review, and elsewhere. She studied music at Harvard University. When not focused on her writing, Emily enjoys reading, hiking, and attending concerts.

If you enjoyed reading her book, please leave a review on Amazon. Reviews are one of the best ways to support authors, and she appreciates hearing from her fans.

INSOMNIA
PUBLISHING

www.insomnia-publishing.com

Made in the USA
Middletown, DE
22 October 2016